ANTISOCIAL HOUSING

Tim Mendees

First Edition
Mythos
Kindlyckevägen 13
Rimforsa, Sweden.
2022

This is a work of fiction. Similarities to real people,
places, or events
Are entirely coincidental

Antisocial Housing by
Tim Mendees
Paperback: 978-91-987509-5-9
Ebook: 978-91-987509-6-6
Cover Design and illustration by
Womba Dream
Formatted by
C. Marry Hultman
Edited by
C. Marry Hultman

www.nordicpresspublishing.com

PREVIOUS WORK BY TIM MENDEES

Fronds: A Cosmic Horror Short Story

Horror for Hire: First Shift

Little Terrors 3:
The Grime of the Ancient Mariner

Boiling Shadow

Carpe Detritus

Burning Reflection

The Pseudopod That Rocks the Cradle

Spiffing

The Creeping Void:
Terror on the Highlands

Miracle Growth

PRAISE FOR ANTISOCIAL HOUSING

- If you love Lovecraft and Poe, you'll surely devour the contemporary and historical horrors contained in ANTISOCIAL HOUSING!

Mallory Anne-Marie H, Reviewer

- It keeps you on the edge of your seat and is very hard to put down. I give this a five star rating.

Alicia M (allis_books)

Antisocial Housing is a great read. This is a worthy addition to the Mendees mythos.

Deborah Dubas Groom (writer)

PART I

Bad Plumbing

I

The television screen flickered with garish light as the mouths of the identikit presenters went up and down like immaculately airbrushed puppets. Mike had completely lost track of what was going on. When he started watching, it had been something soporific about moderately wealthy people buying houses in moderately expensive areas. Now it appeared to be inept pseudo-celebrities trying to wash dogs or shear sheep or something equally inane. Why he bothered paying for the TV license was a mystery.

In the end, it didn't matter what was on. All that Mike could hear was the awful gurgling in the pipes. He had tried turning up the volume, but all that succeeded in doing was to provoke the cantankerous old woman in the flat next door to fly into one of her frequent sub-psychotic rages. She had wailed like a banshee and threatened to report him to the council. Mike had meekly gone along with it and turned it back down. The last thing he needed in his forties was an ASBO. In the end, he turned the sound off and made the vacuous dialogue up in his head.

Current events had conspired to put a massive rotten cherry on top of the newly constructed low-rise flat's myriad problems. Along with the inevitable gaps around the windows, doors that didn't shut properly and lifts that were seemingly possessed by the devil; it looked suspiciously as though the contractors had cut material costs by constructing the walls entirely out of cardboard, and thin cardboard at that. And then... there were the pipes.

For the first few weeks, after he moved into his current abode, everything was peachy. The toilet flushed and the taps ran with clean water. The drains were fast and didn't reek. Everything worked as it should, and nothing was in disrepair. That all changed after a localised earth-tremor sent the plumbing in the building completely out of whack. For over a month now, the toilet had regularly backed up, the taps sputtered, and the drains stank. To top it all off, there was an around the clock din that sounded like an industrial band was recording an experimental album in the water tank.

Mike sighed and took the last bite of his microwaved beef burger. It tasted vaguely of plastic, but he had gotten used to it. He hadn't been one for cooking since his wife walked out on him a year ago. Since that fateful day, he had spent his downtime sitting on his backside stuffing his face with crisps. It had got to the point that he could tell the difference between brands without even glancing at the packet. A sorry state of affairs.

A sharp pinging noise announced that Mike had an email. He groaned as he leaned over and retrieved his laptop from the coffee table. Finally, some good news. The council had replied to his cheesed-off email and were sending 'their best man' to look at the plumbing tomorrow. It probably wouldn't do any good, it never did, but he lived in hope; no matter how vague that hope may be.

His recent diet of junk food and supermarket lager had seen his waistline expand at an alarming rate. He didn't so much have a six-pack as a whole barrel. Getting out of his reclining chair and to his feet took far more effort than it ever should. He grunted involuntarily as he bent over and gathered up the detritus of his most recent binge. He was never quite sure whether it was depression or simple bone-idleness that kept him away from the gym but whatever it was, it was doing a fine job. Laziness, one... willpower, nil.

Screwing up the various wrappers and aluminium cans, Mike shuffled to the postage-stamp-sized kitchen and stuffed them into his overflowing bin. It was well overdue emptying and Mike just knew that the thin plastic liner was going to split. Mike sighed again. That was a problem for another day. There was no way that he was putting any clothes on and going outside. He was perfectly happy in his tatty boxer shorts and stained grey t-shirt, thank you very much.

After opening the fridge door, Mike moved aside a sad-looking lettuce and retrieved another beer. He was getting low again. This meant that he would have to brave the horrors of shopping tomorrow. Yet another sigh escaped his lips as he wondered if life could get any more depressing. It was as though some great cosmic force was having a damn good laugh at his expense.

Mike cracked open the can and grabbed his glass. He was on to the really cheap stuff now and needed to rinse it out. The combination of crap and not-so-crap lagers created a surprisingly horrible concoction that he tried his best to avoid. The froth always went funny and clung to the rim of the glass like scum on a pond. He twisted the tap, but nothing came out. He turned it back off then tried again... Nothing.

Losing his patience, Mike slapped the moulded plastic grip with the flat of his palm.

Splat

A thick gob of foul-smelling goop spat into the stainless-steel sink. It was black and foul with a strange iridescence that gave it an oily texture.

"What the hell?" Mike barked in surprise. He leaned in for a closer look. It was trembling almost imperceptibly. If it wasn't so crazy, he could have sworn that it reacted to his shadow.

The last thing on earth he wanted to do at that moment was to touch the hideous substance that had just spat from his tap, but he couldn't just leave it in the sink. For a start, the overpowering stench was making his eyes water.

Mike wadded up a length of kitchen towel and pressed it down on the filth. It was springy, bouncy, almost jelly-like. It reminded him of the centre of a *Jaffa Cake.* He dragged it towards the plughole and was shocked to see that it left a thick, sticky trail. As he lifted the towel to go back and erase its track, the glob slurped back to its starting position like it hadn't moved at all.

"What?" Mike had never encountered anything so bizarre in all his life. "Get down the damn hole," he swore under his breath as he tried again. With the same infuriating results.

Mike growled in the back of his throat and took a swig of beer directly from the can. He wiped his mouth with the back of his hand and tried once more. This time, he had another wad of paper ready and wiped its trail along with it. "Gotcha," he bellowed in triumph as he lifted the bunched-up tissue and saw that it was finally gone.

As he swigged his beer in celebration, a disgusting gurgle directed his bloodshot eyes to the hole. He slammed the can down and turned the tap again. This time, it worked... eventually. After an unsettling chugging sound, icy-cold water gushed into the shallow sink. It splashed up at Mike, soaking his t-shirt. "Balls," he grumbled. "Bloody perfect. Can life be any more annoying?"

As if to answer his question, the stream of clear water gradually turned a rusty, reddish-brown. It had a distinctly metallic odour to it as it raced towards the plughole.

Woosh

A filthy tongue of strange material burst from the hole. Mike screamed in horror as it rose into the air in front of his face. It was comprised of the same gelid substance as the mystery glob. It throbbed and vibrated as it lengthened, stretched then sharpened to a needle-like point.

Splat

The ooze punctured his eyeball and

slammed into his brain. Mike bellowed in agony as his brain was liquefied. The substance was corrosive. It burned like concentrated acid. In seconds his skull had melted and collapsed in upon itself.

Mike's hands went into spasm. The beer can was crushed in his grip. Beer squirted out of the can and splashed over the walls and floor. His fingers twisted the can, ripping it open. As the fluid continued to dissolve his head, blood poured from his now lacerated hand.

Down his neck it surged, stripping the flesh and melting the sinew. It coursed around his body, consuming his organs and sucking every drop of nutrient from his bones. The monstrous fluid reached Mike's toes in seconds. The skin around his nails split as vile black protoplasm burst forth. It gathered in a growing pool at his feet before surging up the outside of his body.

In seconds, Mike had been completely consumed, clothes and all. The quivering mass of pulsating matter lengthened, sunk in upon itself, trembled, and then shot back down the hole. All trace of Mike had been devoured...

The steady *drip, drip, drip* of the tap and the mangled beer can were the only indication that anything untoward had happened.

II

Paul Cannon frowned as yet another saccharine pop song from a bygone decade burst from the speakers in his white work van. It was the same every morning on every station his rubbish radio could pick up. It was almost as though the various breakfast show disc jockeys were locked in an ongoing battle to out-cheese one another. Right now, this guy was winning. It was so cheesy it nearly triggered Paul's lactose intolerance and sent him racing for the toilet.

Sid sat in the passenger seat tunelessly humming along. Paul was surprised that the young whippersnapper knew it. The damnable track was older than he was. Sid was fresh from school and eager to learn. Well... Eager was probably too strong a word; willing was probably closer.

Paul reached out his calloused fingers and switched the radio off.

"Hey," Sid whined. "I was listening to that." He had one of those fashionable haircuts that were shaved around the sides and short on top. Paul thought it made him look like he had a strip of brown Astroturf glued to his head. Paul, on the other hand, was as bald as a plucked turkey.

"Tough." Paul smiled. "It's my van, my rules, remember? Anyway, it's almost time to go in." They had parked up in the Burridge Court car park on the Edwards Estate. The low-rise block had been thrown up almost overnight, along with the rest of the estate, about five years ago, after the old estate had been bulldozed.

The high-rise block that had stood where Burridge Court stood today, along with its twin down the road, had been considered unsafe. A spate of violent incidents had prompted the council to level the lot and start again.

Unfortunately, the same shoddy building practices that led to the downfall of the old blocks had been used again in the new. Time marches on, but nothing ever truly changes.

Sid sighed and fished a cigarette out of the crumpled carton he had in the breast pocket of his boiler suit and put it in his mouth.

Paul shot him a dirty look.

"I know." Sid sulked. "No smoking in the van. Your van, your rules... Blah, blah, blah..." He opened the door and stepped out into the chilly morning breeze. "What are we going to need out of the back?" he asked after sparking up and taking a deep drag.

"No sodding idea." Paul shrugged, getting out of the van. "I don't know how much we will be able to do. The whole drainage system was installed by Billy the ruddy Kid." He moved around to the back of the van, opened the door and put on his tool belt.

Straightening his back and grunting with pain, Paul moved around to where Sid was sitting on the bonnet playing with his mobile phone.

"Tell you what," he began as a brainwave hit him. "I'll go in and speak to Mr..." he glanced at the worksheet. “Taylor. Once I know what the problem is, I'll give you a ring and you can bring what we need. In the meantime, make sure all the washers and things are in the right slots. We don't want another game of 'hunt the right sized nut' do we?” Paul was referring to a previous disaster when all the nuts, bolts, screws and washers ended up in a big pick-and-mix in the bottom of the toolbox.

“Right. Will do.” Sid replied airily. This was one of the many problems Paul had with the youngster. He was never sure if he was on this planet. Paul blamed all the dope he obviously smoked going by the smell of his clothes.

Paul grunted and started to walk towards the building before turning.

“Oh, Sid.”

“Yeah?" Sid didn't even look up from his frantic messaging. He always had at least one girl on the go; Paul didn't know how he managed it.

“Get your arse off the bonnet, there's a good lad. The suspension is knackered enough without your fifteen stone rump perched on it,”

Sid huffed and stood up. Paul chuckled

to himself and walked off. There was nothing wrong with the suspension, he just liked needling the sullen youth... It's the little things that make a day bearable.

***

Police Sergeant Gary Fisher had been on the force for nearly thirty years. He had started his career in Truro but was moved to his native Betyls Cove after an unfortunate incident involving a superior officer's fingers and a car door. Fisher had always maintained that it had been an accident but top brass wasn't buying it. The move was seen as a punishment, but Fisher knew full well that his hometown had more than its fair share of meaty cases. Plus, the commute along the torturous A-roads was always a massive pain in the rear.

As he pulled into the car park, his partner, PC Granger, asked, "What's the call?" Charlotte Granger was a young probationer who had been put with Fisher to learn some old tricks from the old dog.

"We got a couple of complaints last night from Mrs Travis," Fisher began.

Granger rolled her eyes. Even this early in

her career she knew a serial complainant when she met one.

“First was about her neighbour's TV. Then about an hour later she rang again saying that the guy was screaming and shouting. She reckoned she believed he was going to come and beat her up. The poor sod probably just stubbed his toe or something...”

“Yeah, she complained about the postman hammering her door *aggressively* the other day.” Granger chuckled.

“That sounds about right.” Fisher smiled and pulled on the handbrake. “Still, we have to follow up on everything. No matter how bat-shit-crazy the complainant is.” He grabbed his hat off the dashboard. “Come on... Let's get this over with.”

The two officers stepped out of the marked car and walked to the front of the building. Burridge Court was four stories high and comprised of one rectangular block. Each flat had a small balcony and was of the same size whether it had one or two bedrooms. The front door had an electronic panel next to it with state-of-the-art locking systems. The door was opened using an electronic key-fob. Fisher and

Granger didn't have one of those so they would have to call Mrs Travis using the keypad and intercom. Fisher punched in her flat number and waited...

"Hello? What do you want?" A shrill voice answered.

"Mrs Travis?" Fisher inquired, though he knew exactly who he was talking to. "It's the police... About your complaints... Last night."

"How do I know it's the police? You could be anyone," a note of hysteria entered Mrs Travis' voice. "I don't keep any money in the flat."

Fisher sighed. "Mrs Travis, it's me, Gary Fisher. You went to school with my mum."

"Ooh yes." Mrs Travis cooed. "Hehe. She was a wild one."

Fisher muttered something unpleasant under his breath, then asked. "Can we come in?"

"Yes, dear. Come on up."

Fisher and Granger looked at each other as the seconds ticked by.

"Can you press the buzzer then?" Fisher asked, desperately trying to keep his temper in check.

“Ooh, of course, dear. Silly me..."

Buzz

“Hold the door,” a voice called out as they opened it.

Fisher looked around. “Oh. Hi, Paul. You got a job on?”

Paul held out his hand. “Yeah, up on third. Some guy's pipes are knackered. What are you two doing here?” He shook Gary's hand, then held it up as a salute. “Hi, Caroline.”

“Mrs Travis," Fisher replied. "The usual..."

“Ahh, say no more.” Paul smiled. “I had to fit a tap for her a couple of months back... That was fun.”

“I can well imagine.” Fisher snorted.

The trio walked into the lobby, nearly skidding on the vast collection of fast-food menus that had been shoved under the door. Upon reaching the lift, Granger jabbed the call button.

“Going up?” she asked Paul.

“Yeah. I'm going to the flat next door to Mrs Travis. A guy called Mike. You probably know him, Gary. He plays darts for the Ancient Mariner.” Paul stepped into the lift first and hit the third-floor button.

As the door squeaked and shuddered as it closed, Fisher turned to Granger. "That probably explains all the shouting. The guy was just swearing at the pipes."

"Eh?" Paul cocked an eyebrow.

"Mrs Travis complained about him shouting last night... That's why we're here." Granger clarified.

Ding

The lift doors opened onto the third-floor landing. The long corridor smelt of paint and silicon sealant. It was completely bare except for a rusty bicycle down one end. Motion sensors picked up their movements as they left the lift and switched the lights on. The bare bulbs reflected harshly off the council's standard eggshell paint. It felt like being in a nineteen-sixties hospital. Both flats were down the far end with two more opposite.

"I'll see you in a bit then, Paul." Fisher grinned. "We'll be round to speak to Mike when we are done here."

Paul nodded and knocked on Mike's door.

Granger pressed Mrs Travis' doorbell and after a moment the door opened just a fraction. The chain was securely fastened, and a piercing blue eye squinted through the gap. Once she was sure that they were who they said they were, she shut the door, slid off the chain then opened it again.

"Come in, quickly," she hissed urgently. Two large cats tried to push their way past her legs, but Fisher blocked their escape. He knew the drill by now, he had been there enough times.

"Hello, Jasper. Hello, Ollie." He said to the cats as he held them back so Granger could slip inside.

Granger almost retched as the overwhelming smell of ammonia delivered a knockout blow to her gag reflex. It was so powerful that it made her eyes water. Fisher moved through into the lounge, and already Mrs Travis was in full flow.

"It's just not right, is it? Shouting and bawling at all hours of the day or night. Doors slamming. Television loud enough to wake the dead. No consideration for anyone but himself." Her words came out in a staccato burst that could have been fired from an AK-47. She didn't even pause for breath when she lowered herself into her armchair.

“I have a weak heart, you know? All this noise and carrying on, it's just not good enough. It plays hell with Jasper's nerves. Doesn't it boy?” She scooped the overfed lump of black fur off the carpet and started to coo at it. The cat looked confusedly at his marmalade pal who shifted furtively away from the chair and behind Fisher's legs.

Using this break in her rant, Fisher asked, “So, what exactly happened last night?”

“I just told you,” Mrs Travis barked indignantly. “First he turned his television up so loud that I could hear every word. Celebrities shearing sheep... I ask you? I banged on the wall and told him to turn it down. Then, about an hour later, he starts screaming bloody murder. I feared for my life, I did. Properly raising Cain, he was.”

The sound of banging from the corridor distracted Fisher for a moment. A fact that was picked up by their eagle-eyed and rapier-tongued host. “See,” Mrs Travis yelled. “There he goes again. Banging and crashing around. It's enough to drive a person doolally. Isn't it, Jasper?” The cat purred lazily and rolled his big orange eyes.

Fisher held up his hand like a child in a classroom. "No. I think that's the plumber. Your neighbour has been having trouble with his pipes. I think that's what a lot of the banging is..."

“Nonsense,” Mrs Travis hissed. Cutting off Fisher's sentence. “They’re all the same, his sort. Thugs an’ hooligans, the lot of ‘em.”

Fisher bristled and turned sharply away, desperately trying to hold his tongue. “Take her statement, Granger,” he shouted over his shoulder as he left the room. “I'm going to see what all the commotion is about.”

As he reached the front door, Fisher was joined by a pair of stampeding cats. He managed to keep them inside as he slipped out. He couldn't help feeling sorry for the poor creatures. “I feel for you guys, I really do. I'd be trying to make a run for it too. But...” he sighed ruefully, “The old devil would be after my job if I let you out.”

Pulling the door closed behind him, Fisher turned and spoke to Paul, who was *still* banging on the door. “What's going on? Isn't he in?”

“I'm starting to worry.” Paul shook his head and pointed at the keyhole. “The key's in the lock. You can see here..." He pointed to the edge of the door. It was so poorly hung that the bolt was visible. "The bolt's on. So, he either jumped out of the window or..."

Fisher moved towards the door. "Have you tried shouting through the letterbox?"

"That brings me to my next point..." Paul put his hand over his mouth as Fisher lifted the flap.

"Jesus wept," Fisher gagged as a putrid smell escaped from the aperture.

"Bad isn't it?" Paul asked rhetorically. "It smells like something has died."

Fisher shuddered. He was only too aware as to what it smelled like. Though, if Mike was alive and well the previous evening, what was causing the stench? A body doesn't smell like that overnight. Horrible memories of reading about the Nilsen, Dahmer and Gacy murder cases raced through his mind. "I'm going to have to kick it down. The guy might need medical attention."

"Smells like he is well past medical attention," Paul grimaced.

Fisher would have to agree, though, he kept his thoughts to himself. "Stand back, Paul.

I'm going to kick it in."

Standing as yet another testament to the shoddy finishing on display at Burridge Court, the door put up little resistance to Fisher's size thirteen police-issue boot. The hinges gave way and the door came loose. After a bit of jiggling, Fisher was able to release the bolt and move the door aside.

"You'd better keep back, Paul," Fisher instructed, adjusting his hat. "Mike? Can you hear me?" He shouted then quickly clamped his mouth shut. The smell was revolting. It hung in the air like a miasma. He rummaged in his pockets and pulled out a pair of plastic gloves and a handkerchief. Mike hadn't replied to any of their attempts at communication. Fisher feared the worst.

The flat was completely silent except for the drip of the kitchen tap. Fisher poked his head around the bathroom and bedroom doors then moved into the living room. Confusion washed over him as he found it completely empty once again. There was only one more place to look... The kitchen.

Nearing the door, the stench became almost unbearable. Fisher had to fight the nausea that was rising in his gorge. It took all of his strength not to dash outside for some fresh air. He gently pushed the door. It creaked on its wonky hinges as it opened to reveal... Nothing. Well, nearly nothing.

At first glance, everything seemed to be in order. Upon closer scrutiny, however, Fisher noticed some disturbing evidence... The torn, mangled and bloody beer can. It had fallen just next to the fridge. Several spatters of blood stood out in grisly contrast to the plain white appliance. Fisher crouched down and examined the can. Mangled lumps of Mike's flesh were stuck to the jagged edges, thick lumps. It was no wonder the guy was screaming.

Though there was no cadaver to be seen, it was clear to Fisher that something ghastly had happened to Mike. Looking around, he discovered the source of the smell. Leaning over the sink, he was hit full in the face by the foul aroma. He leaned over and opened the window. Greedily gulping down the fresh air, Fisher steadied himself against the worktop

Gurgle

Fisher jumped as a disgusting sound belched forth from the plughole. It was a sucking, squelching noise that sounded unnervingly like someone sucking chicken off the bone. Fisher backed away instinctively and walked back into the lounge.

Throwing the windows wide, Fisher stood next to the television, which was still on, and pondered the situation. The owner of the flat had seemingly vanished into thin air. It was almost like one of those *locked-room mysteries* that he used to read as a child. Something had obviously occurred, the gory beer can proved that... Then there was the sink. There was something *very* wrong with the plumbing... It's a good job he had an expert on hand.

III

Mrs Travis had almost exploded with rage when she heard Fisher kick her neighbour's door down. Granger thought for a second that her head was going to start spinning around. It took all of her police training to calm the woman down. She had finally stopped screeching when Fisher hammered on the door.

"What the hell is happening," she bawled. "Oh, my poor heart," she grasped her chest dramatically. Despite all her bluster to the contrary, her last check-up revealed her to be as strong as an ox.

"Calm down, Mrs Travis. It's only Sergeant Fisher." Granger stood up sharply, truly grateful for the escape hatch her colleague had provided. She deftly evaded the feline escape artists and let Fisher inside. One look at his haggard face told her that something was wrong.

"Can you try your radio?" Fisher asked without any preamble. "I can't get anything on mine... Just static."

Granger unclipped her radio from her belt and pressed the call button. "PC Granger to control. Can you read me? Over."

Crackle

"PC Granger to control. Come in, control... Over." She gave the device a shake for good luck.

Hiss

"PC Granger to control. Do you read..."

Tekeli-li

The harsh noise nearly made Granger throw the radio across the corridor in surprise. "What the hell?"

"Mine's the same," Fisher said solemnly. He cursed and put his mobile phone back into his vest pocket. "No bloody signal either. How's yours?"

Granger looked at her phone and shook

her head. “Not a sausage, Sarge.”

Fisher poked his head into the living room. “Do you have a landline, Mrs Travis?”

“You must be joking?” the belligerent pensioner barked in outrage. “I saw one of those programs on the television. Only people after your personal details use phones nowadays. I'm not having some scoundrel stealing my identity...”

Fisher closed the living-room door on her in full flow. Not that she noticed. He could hear her clucking away to her cats. “Bugger...” He pondered for a second. “Okay, I'll go outside and use the payphone around the corner. We need to get CID in here.”

Granger raised a perfectly shaped eyebrow. “It's serious then?”

“Seriously bloody weird," Fisher grumbled. "The guy has vanished from a room on the third floor that was locked from the inside and the only trace is a mangled beer-can with bits of the guy's fingers stuck to it... Like I said... Bloody weird."

“What should I do then, sarge?” Granger asked, dreading the answer.

“Take her statement... I know... I know.

Try and get the time of the screams off her at least." Fisher stepped back outside while Granger held back the cats. "Oh, Granger?"

"Sarge?" She replied sulkily.

"Try not to kill her and feed her to the cats." Fisher chuckled and shut the door.

Granger muttered under her breath. This wasn't going to be fun. Mrs Travis was still ranting about phones. She was on to the thorny subject of heavy breathing perverts now. Granger let out a heavy sigh and went back into the living room.

***

Paul jabbed his phone with his forefinger then gave up and put it back into his pocket. Fisher took one look at his face and didn't have to ask how his signal was. "Right," Fisher began. "I'm going to try the phone box around the corner. I want to take a look at those pipes... Do you have what you need in your van?"

"Yeah. I'll come down with you and grab what I need. It should be pretty standard stuff." Paul smiled, desperately attempting to hide the simple fact that he had no desire whatsoever to go into Mike's reeking abode.

Paul jabbed the call button on the lift. The gears made an unnerving grinding sound followed by a large *clunk*... "Perfect," Fisher spat. "Looks like we are taking the stairs."

"Who built this bloody place?" Paul huffed. "Laurel and sodding Hardy?"

The heavy fire-door to the staircase slammed shut behind them, momentarily plunging them into darkness. After a few seconds, the sensor picked them up and the sickly yellow lights flickered into life.

The two men took the stairs down to the ground floor in silence. Fisher's brain was fully occupied with trying to connect the dots. The only place that Mike could have possibly gone, based on the evidence at hand, was down the plughole... But that was impossible... Wasn't it?

Whichever moron had wired the motion sensors for the lights had spaced them too far apart and put the timer on for far too short a time. Every time they reached a landing, the lights went out. Fisher walked into the bannister on two occasions and Paul snagged his shirt on a door handle... Today wasn't going so well. In fact, it was slowly turning into a nightmare.

When they reached the first-floor landing,

a sudden *pop* announced that they had yet more trouble to contend with.

"What now?" Fisher snarled as the lights went off and the building fell silent.

"Power cut, I think." Paul took out his phone and switched on the flashlight. "You get them all the time on the Edwards Estate. Council was supposed to fix the grid but..." He let the sentence hang.

"That sounded like something blew, though" Fisher pointed out.

"True. It could be the breakers. If the wiring is anything like the plumbing, then I ain't touching 'em. The last thing I need is a few thousand volts up my backside."

Fisher chuckled at that. Finally, they reached the bottom and stepped out into the foyer. The front door had glass panels so at least they had a little bit of light. Paul went to press the door release switch and let out a string of expletives.

"What's up?" Fisher looked at Paul like he had just fallen off the moon.

"Sodding door's electric." Paul fumed. "We are locked in."

"There has to be a way to open it. In

emergencies, I mean," Fisher scratched his cranium.

"There is." Paul pointed to a keyhole. "Got the key?"

Fisher shook his head.

"Nope. Me neither. Not on me, anyway."

"We will have to use a fire exit or something." A peeling poster on the wall indicated the exits. Fisher screwed his eyes up to try and see through the elaborate graffiti tags and doodles of male genitals that covered eighty per cent of the diagram.

"Hold on." Paul had spotted a forlorn figure next to the door. It was Sid. He was currently leaning on a drainpipe, smoking a fag and fiddling with his phone. "I've got one of the keys in the van. The council gave me a set for jobs in vacant units. Sid can get it for us... Hey, Sid." Paul banged on the window shaking Sid out of his latest daydream.

Sid mouthed "What?" in a miserable fashion in response.

"Get the keyring out of the van."

Sid shrugged.

"The keyring. Go and get it from the van," Paul over-enunciated every word.

Sid couldn't lip read. He shrugged again.

Paul took out his car keys and jingled them about in front of the window then pointed at the van.

Sid looked at the keys, looked at the van, then shrugged.

Paul was about to explode when Fisher pointed out the letterbox. “Talk through that.” He gave a little chuckle at both men's stupidity. Paul didn't hear it, thankfully, he was too annoyed with himself.

“Can you hear me now?” Paul said through the flap.

“Just about," Sid replied.

“Come over here then,” Paul demanded.

Sid took one step forward then stopped.

Paul and Fisher looked on in confusion as Sid's back foot, his left, refused to move from the grid that it was resting upon. It looked like someone had glued him to the spot.

Sid hopped around for a better position then tried to drag his leg off the grate. As he strained and pulled, a sticky, tar-like substance came with it. It was stuck to his trainer and sucked his foot back down to the ground with a disgusting *slurp*. He tried again with the same perplexing result. Sid looked on in astonishment as the sole of his running shoe melted into the black ooze, giving it a white stripe for a brief second.

Sid's body jerked in agony as the protoplasm engulfed his foot. He screamed, hopped and waved his arms but he just couldn't get free.

Fisher and Paul looked on in horrified amazement as the liquid climbed up his leg. It was now a shimmering mass of pulsing fluid up to just past his knee. The fluid pulled and Sid's leg snapped like a twig. His body toppled forwards and was soon grabbed by more of the foul substance. It wrapped itself around his torso and sucked him dry. Sid had died, mercifully, moments ago. Soon his body was utterly dissolved.

Once all trace of Sid had gone, the creature in the drain rose into an undulating mound outside the door. Hundreds of hateful orange eyes snapped open on its bulk and glared hungrily at Fisher and Paul.

"Holy shit," Fisher cried in terror. "What the fuck is that thing?"

Paul didn't answer... Paul couldn't. He was

too busy vomiting in a corner.

The creature shuddered in something akin to laughter then flattened into a bubbling puddle and started to creep towards the door.

Fisher grabbed Paul by the shoulder and dragged him towards the stairs. The puddle was coming *under* the door. It had made short work of the bristles that acted as a draft excluder. Already a tennis-ball-sized glob had formed on the welcome mat.

Tekeli-li

The thing shrieked and piped. It was the same shrill sound that had emitted from Fisher's police radio. As he yanked open the door to the staircase, a three-lobed eye appeared on the glob and followed their movement. Fisher took the torch off his utility belt and lit the darkened staircase.

"What?" Paul yammered, "What was that *thing*?" His voice cracked. "Poor Sid..."

Fisher panted, he wasn't as young or in as good shape as he used to be, he was far too fond of pasties and ale to keep in trim. "I have no idea. We need to get Granger and find a phone. Then we need to get everyone out of here."

Paul was far too shaken to question the logic of going *up,* he just followed the veteran copper in stunned silence.

***

PC Granger dunked her pink wafer into her cup of anaemic tea while the two cats fussed around her legs. Mrs Travis had calmed down sufficiently enough that she had been able to get the facts down in her notebook. She had graciously accepted the offer of tea and biscuits and listened to the old lady ramble on. It was a mercy when the tea moved through her system and she had to go to the little girl's room... The last five minutes had been relatively peaceful.

She tried the radio yet again. All she got was the same static screech as before. It was at that certain pitch that made her teeth itch. The power had gone down a few minutes before. Granger was pleasantly surprised when Mrs Travis had shrugged it off as one of those unavoidable things. She had expected her to go into total meltdown. If you are going to settle down in a small town in Cornwall, then you have to expect the odd blackout and wonky phone coverage.

The silence was shattered by the flushing of the toilet. Granger put the cup and saucer aside and took out her notebook. Suddenly, a soul shrivelling scream came from the bathroom.

“Help," Mrs Travis bawled at the top of her lungs. "Help me, please. Something is pulling me down the toilet."

The two cats leapt behind the sofa and hid under the TV stand. Granger jumped to her feet and raced to the bathroom. The door was closed but not locked. She twisted the knob and let the door swing open.

Mrs Travis was up to her armpits in the toilet bowl. Granger nearly collapsed from the shock and grabbed onto the doorframe to steady herself.

“Don't just stand there, help me,” Mrs Travis demanded. Her arms were flailing wildly. Granger grabbed one of them and pulled with all her might.

Slurp

The arm came away from the socket. The skin stretched and blackened. Mrs Travis gave out one final scream before her head was dragged into the bowl. Granger crashed into a full-length mirror as the arm waved around violently in the air. It was connected to the bubbling organism in the toilet by a thick black tentacle.

As shards of mirror-glass tinkled to the tiles, the wizened hand of Mrs Travis stretched out its bony fingers for PC Granger, they stretched and grasped at the air just inches from her face. She scrambled backwards and pulled herself up on the towel-rail as the arm tentacle swung towards her head.

With one deft flick of the wrist, Granger had her police-baton fully extended. Swinging wildly, she cracked the hand right in the knuckles the fingers twisted and bent under the force of the blow. Swinging again, she managed to ward the tentacle off. It slammed into the shower cubicle, spilling toiletries all over the floor.

The toilet gurgled as a massive column of rippling ooze grew out of the bowl. One huge orange eye glared at Granger.

Tekeli-li

Granger darted from the room and slammed the door. She could hear the creature thrashing around, smashing the fittings and cracking the tiles. It must have smashed the sink to oblivion as water began to gush from multiple broken pipes. She stood staring at the door until the frantic clawing of the cats brought her back to earth.

“Yes, I'm coming.” She yelled and sprinted to the front door. She flung it wide. “Go. Get the hell out of here,” she told the grateful moggies. They raced down the corridor and into Mike's flat through the broken door. The fresh breeze coming from the window had guided them to their escape. Using the balconies, they worked their way around to the north side. From there it was a short leap to a nearby tree. After scrambling down the trunk, they sped off into the estate.

Slamming the door to Mrs Travis' flat behind her, Granger started to make her way down the corridor. As she passed Gary's flat, the door next to it opened and a concerned man in his mid-thirties poked his head around the door.

“What's going on?” The man asked.

Granger didn't have time to answer the man's damn fool questions. "Do you have a landline?" She barked.

The man was startled. “Um, no... Sorry.”

“Bollocks,” Granger spat. “Get inside and stay the hell away from the drains.”

“What?”

Before she could elaborate, another voice called from inside the flat. “Chris Help.”

Granger and the man, Chris, looked at each other then raced inside.

“It's Richey," Chris explained. "He's taking a shower."

Granger groaned. She knew by the screams what was happening in the bathroom. She and Chris burst in to see poor Richey under the shower. Only it wasn't fine jets of water that were coming out of the head... It was more of the murderous ooze.

It had gushed down onto his naked body in thin rivulets. His skin was bubbling and dissolving before their eyes. Chris grabbed his lover by the arm and tried to drag him clear, but he was held fast by a viscous puddle that had bubbled out of the plughole.

“You can't save him,” Granger yelled at the distraught man, but it was too late. Several of the thin strands from the showerhead had woven themselves into a ropey tendril. With a sharp *crack*, it snapped towards Chris. He didn't even have time to scream before it had coiled around his neck and throttled him. He collapsed into the shower and both men were quickly smothered.

Granger ran for her life. Through the living room and out into the corridor where she nearly swung for Fisher's skull with her baton. He caught her and directed her away.

"Jesus Christ," Fisher cried in alarm. "Watch it, You nearly took my bloody head off."

"Sorry, sarge." Granger panted as she crashed into the opposing wall and bent double. Her body shook violently as the adrenaline of near-death coursed around her veins. She pointed a shaky finger at the door she had just fallen out of and tried to force words through the hyperventilation.

Fisher put his huge paw on her shoulder and shook his head. "I think I know what you just saw... Big sludgy thing covered in eyes?"

Granger nodded with wide questioning eyes.

"We saw it... It... Ate Sid." Paul sniffed back the tears. He might have been a lazy so and so, but he was *his* lazy so and so. Paul had liked Sid tremendously.

"Yeah," Granger started after recovering control of her body. "It got Mrs Travis and the two blokes in there. What the fuck is it, sarge?"

"God alone knows. What I do know, is that it's some kind of creature... We need to clear the building and call in the army or something. I mean, how the hell can we stop a *thing* that can hide in the pipes and trickle under doors? It's not the sort of thing you can just call *Rentokil* for. I doubt even the army can stop it, but we have got to try," Fisher pointed down the corridor. "Let's start here and work our way down. We can take a door each, it'll save time."

The others agreed and each headed towards one of the remaining six doors on the landing. The evacuation of Burridge Court had begun.

IV

Barry exhaled the pungent smoke and passed the uncommonly fat spliff to his friend, Kyle. His eyes rolled up into his skull as the powerful THC worked its magic on his frazzled brain.

"Hey, Barry. Did you hear that, dude?" Kyle asked between puffs.

"Hear what?"

"All that screaming and crashing around."

Barry thought for a few seconds longer than it should have taken to formulate a response. "Oh. A minute ago, you mean?"

"Yeah. Sounded like world war three." Kyle coughed and reached for his bottle of energy drink. The one drawback to this current mind-bending strain of hybrid weed was that it left you with a mouth like the Sahara Desert: that and the smell. It smelt like someone had set fire to a cabbage that thirteen cats had urinated on.

"I think it was the two dudes in twenty-four having another domestic." Barry graciously took the joint from his friend and had a good toke.

Kyle nodded; his friend's theory was not only plausible but also had a solid grounding in fact. Chris and Richey had enjoyed a somewhat stormy relationship. It wasn't uncommon to hear raised voices coming from their unit. They were both really nice guys, but they didn't half bicker.

Thump, Thump, Thump,

"Who is it?" Kyle answered the banging on the door without thinking.

"Shut up, man," Barry hissed. "It might be debt collectors."

"Eh?" Kyle glared at his flat mate. "You did pay the TV license, didn't you?"

"Um..." Barry looked sheepish.

Thump, Thump, Thump,

"For fuck's sake, Barry. You can go to prison for not paying that."

Thump, Thump, Thump,

This time, the knocking was accompanied by the irritated voice of police sergeant Fisher. "Open up. I know you're in there... I heard you whispering. It's the police... Open up."

"Oh shit," Kyle whispered. "It's the filth."

"What do we do?" Barry asked, his face turning deathly pale.

"You stash the weed. I'll open the door." Kyle stood up.

"Wait," Barry called after him. "He'll smell it."

"So what? You can have a bit for personal use but an ounce ain't classed as personal... I'm not going to jail for possession with intent... Stash it in the cistern and let me deal with it."

Barry hauled himself off the pizza-stained sofa and scooped up the big bag of stinky weed and slipped into the bathroom and locked the door behind him. Kyle gave him a few minutes then stood up.

Kyle blew the air away from the door and wafted his hands around in the air; like that was going to make a damn bit of difference.

He took a deep breath and opened it. “Hello?”

Fisher's face was as red as a beetroot. “You need to come with us...”

“What?” Kyle yelped. “You can't... It's just a bit of puff.”

Fisher grabbed him by the shoulder and yanked him into the corridor. “I'm not here about your bloody weed. Where's Chong?”

“Who?” Kyle scratched his head.

“*You're* Cheech, *he's* Chong and *we* need to get the hell out of the building.”

Kyle chuckled like a buffoon. “Cheech and Chong... I get it now.”

“We don't have time for this shit, Kyle. Is Barry in or not?” Fisher was rapidly losing patience.

“Uh... Yeah... He just went to the bathroom...”

“Oh no.” Fisher barged past him and hammered on the bathroom door... He got no answer. “Barry, come out of there now. I don't care about the stash you *aren't* hiding in the cistern... Just get out of there now.”

Again... There was no reply.

Fisher reared back on his left leg and booted the door open. There were water, blood and marijuana everywhere. Barry's feet were sticking out of the back of the toilet. Fisher had seen enough. He turned and raced out of the flat.

"What's going on?" Kyle whined. "Where's Barry?"

Granger and Fisher shared glances; Fisher shook his head. "Fill him in will you, constable?"

Granger nodded and pulled Kyle aside. Fisher joined Paul at the next door.

"Nobody home?" He asked, hoping.

"Dunno. I thought I heard someone moving around a moment ago."

"Here, let me try." He hammered on the door with his fist. "Open up. Police." He put his ear to the door and listened. All he could hear was the gurgling from the pipes in Kyle's flat. It was getting louder with each passing moment. "I don't think anyone's at home." He smiled at Paul. "Come on, let's go down to the next floor.

Tekeli-li

With an almighty *crash*, the huge ball of hungry hate smashed through the door, and wall, of Kyle's flat. It slammed into the wall opposite, just metres from Kyle and Granger, making the building shake. It rippled, spread, then reformed into an iridescent sphere. Hundreds of baleful orange eyes snapped open and glared at the four people in front of it.

Tekeli-li,

“What the hell is that?” Kyle bellowed hysterically.

“Shut up and run,” Granger demanded.

“Run? Run where? It's a dead-end,” Paul screamed.

Tentacles and other loathsome appendages spawned at will from the gelatinous bulk. It trembled with hunger and started to rush towards them piping furiously.

Seconds before they were devoured, the door to number nineteen opened and a thin, dishevelled women poked her head around the door. “Cover your eyes,” She yelled.

All four of them did as they were told and the woman ripped open a kilo bag of salt with her teeth and lobbed it at the incoming creature. It burst on contact and showered the beast. It screamed and recoiled. The salt sizzled and hissed on its body. It thrashed around in agony, its tentacles waving like crazy. One of them slammed through the roof directly above it, bringing plaster and masonry down on its body.

"Quick," The woman shouted. "Inside,"

None of them needed telling twice. They piled through the door while the creature slammed its massive hide against the wall, cracking the plaster.

"Away from the door," The woman ordered. They rushed through into the lounge and stood in awe. The walls were covered in glyphs, charms and formulae. Every free space was covered in a spidery scrawl of an unknown language.

"Well..." Fisher's mouth hung open.

"Great," Kyle spat. "We're trapped in crazy Sarah's house,"

Paul peered down the corridor. Sarah was holding a talisman up to the door and chanting. He came back into the room and shrugged.

Moments later, Sarah came into the room with her eyes wild and her hair even wilder. She was only in her late twenties, but her appearance gave her the look of a crazed old crone. Her arms were covered in home-made tattoos and painful-looking brands all depicting the same five-pointed star design that covered the walls. It was no wonder the locals called her 'crazy' Sarah.

“It's okay you are safe in here," Sarah said in a preternaturally calm voice. "It can't get through my protective spells."

Fisher cocked an eyebrow. “Thanks, Sarah... But spells?”

Kyle snorted derisively.

Sarah shot him a look that could kill a man at twenty paces. “The ancient sign of the Elder Gods.” She pointed at one of the strange stars with a flame-like squiggle in the centre. “It's the only thing that can stop a shoggoth.”

Fisher, Granger and Paul all asked “shoggoth?” in perfect unison.

“That thing out there.” Sarah scurried to the kitchen and took several bags of salt out of her cupboard and lined them up next to the sink. “Take one of these.” She ordered. “If it tries to come up the pipes, empty that down it. It doesn't like salt... As you saw.”

“Like a big slug?” Paul mused aloud, taking one of the bags.

“Precisely.” Sarah nodded and busied past them into the bathroom. She had already made a large stack of bags of salt next to the toilet her brow creasing. “Which is strange since they originate in the sea… must be something to do with the concentration… yes, yes, that must be it.” She smiled and nodded to herself. “Yes. They will be quite safe... For a while... Long enough... Maybe.”

“Sarah?" Fisher asked as she continued to ferret around muttering to herself about curses and talismans. "You seem to know what that thing is?"

“Shoggoth, yes.” She said. “A force from the dawn of time. It has been trapped under Betyls Cove for centuries. Until...”

“Until?” Fisher prompted.

Kyle snorted again at this point. “I can't believe that you are listening to the town loony.”

“Shut the fuck up, Kyle,” Paul hissed, getting right in the young stoner's face. “You explain that creature out there then... You can't can you? No? So keep your mouth shut.”

Sarah smiled the smile of the correctly proven. "You have all called me crazy for warning about the things that lie below this cesspit of a town... Now, look. I was right all along. Who's *crazy* now?"

Kyle rolled his eyes. "You. Still you"

Paul grabbed him by the stained video game t-shirt and jammed his knotted fist in his face. "I swear to god, Kyle. If you don't shut your gob, I'll knock your teeth down your throat. Just shut up and let her talk."

PC Granger moved between the two bickering men. "Boys, boys. Calm down... Now." Her eyes flashed. She was only around five-foot-five but was a black-belt in one of the more esoteric martial arts. They knew this... They shut up and skulked off into opposing corners to sulk like scolded brats.

"Go on, Sarah," Fisher said calmly. "You were saying, until?"

Sarah pulled a green star-shaped stone out of her pocket and placed it on a writing desk near the balcony. The desk was piled high with papers and old journals. "Until *we* disturbed the wards." She looked sullen. Guilt danced in her brown eyes.

"We?" Fisher prompted.

"Professors Winkleman, Crabtree and I." She paused to wet her lips. "When the old tower block was torn down a tunnel was discovered under the foundations. It was ancient. Pre-Roman. We were called in. I was studying archaeology in Truro with Winkleman. There was a whole bunch of us, undergrads, there, digging and cataloguing. It was Winkleman who broke the seal... He didn't know. That *thing* escaped... So many dead... We thought we had trapped it; sealed it up again... We were wrong. Whoever built this place must have disturbed the Elder sign... must have." Her eyes drifted to the table and fixed on a strange carved object. "It's all my fault." She whispered. "If only I had listened to Crabtree... All my fault." Her voice had become a barely audible whisper.

Fisher scratched his head. "So, what can we do to stop it? If that thing gets out..." He let that one hang. It really didn't bear thinking about.

"You have to seal it back in its pit. Everything you need to know is in Crabtree's journal." She indicated a tatty exercise book on her desk.

"You'll help us, right?" Granger asked. "I mean, you know about this *shoggoth* thing."

Sarah opened the balcony door and took a deep lungful of air. She turned and smiled. "I'm afraid not... This is all my fault... I must atone for my sins."

Before anyone could move to stop her, Sarah took a majestic swan-dive off the balcony and crashed to the concrete below. Fisher looked down and winced; there wasn't a chance in hell that she survived the fall.

After the expected hysterics amongst the group had waned, Fisher sat down at the desk and opened Crabtree's journal.

"Now what?" Kyle asked sullenly.

"Now." Fisher asserted. "We see what Professor Crabtree has to say for himself."

PART 2

The Narrative Of Professor Crabtree

V

I'd never even heard of Betyls Cove until I received that fateful email in mid-July. My name is Professor Richard Crabtree and this document is a full and factual account of the horrific events that transpired in the ancient tunnels under the Edwards Estate redevelopment. I am a tenured professor of archaeology at Exeter University and I was leading a dig out in the wilds of Exmoor when I received word from an old colleague, and sparring partner, one Professor Winkleman.

One of my more promising students, an academically bright twenty-one-year-old called Craig, who, unfortunately, was something of a chump when it came to anything practical, came puffing and panting down from the road. He had returned on my instruction to his car with my laptop. From there he had driven around looking for a wireless signal so he could send an email on my behalf to my long-suffering wife. She was well used to me being away for extended periods but understandably expected me to at least tell her that I hadn't kicked the bucket from time to time.

Upon Craig's red-faced return, he conveyed to me an urgent request to get in contact with Professor Winkleman at Truro university. Winkleman had: *Made an earth-shattering discovery.* I had known Dave Winkleman for many years and had never before known him to give himself over to excitable hyperbole. He wanted me to join him at a small fishing port on the Cornish coast. What's more, the presumptuous old devil had been in contact with the faculty at Exeter and had cleared it with them for me to take a working sabbatical from lectures.

I was scheduled to have wrapped up the business of the Exmoor dig by the following Sunday so I sent poor Craig puffing and panting back up the hill to the car with another message. This one was to inform Professor Winkleman that I would promptly drive over the border to Truro on completion of the current project and join him in his rainbow chasing. I also asked him to provide me with a real bed for at least one night, as my creaking bones were getting far too old for extended periods of camping.

Once I had finished at the dig and had dropped my team of undergrads and equipment back to Exeter, I popped home to see my wife and have the first square meal I had eaten in weeks. I used this time to do some research into my upcoming destination. Amongst some wild legends and mystical mumbo-jumbo about Druidic places of power, I discovered some interesting titbits about the Edwards Estate.

The much-needed Edwards Estate redevelopment began in earnest in June of 2018, though the plans had been in place for far longer. Back in 2014, plans to demolish the two towering ten-floor death-traps were quickly drawn up then left buried under a mountain of red tape for four years.

For many reasons, the shoddily built and wildly unsafe structures had become a virtual *'no go zone'* for the citizens of Betyls Cove. The twin cinder-block monstrosities were thrown up, almost overnight, back in the nineteen-sixties, along with a huge sprawl of equally poorly constructed houses. They had been crumbling ever since. Many of the houses had become derelict and bulldozed for public safety. Many thought that the towers were one strong Cornish wind away from joining them.

It wasn't just the safety aspect that hastened their demise; reports of fires, muggings, rapes and even murders had risen sharply since the turn of the century, giving the Edwards Estate the unenviable distinction of being the most violent locale in Cornwall. The catalogue of human misery wasn't purely limited to violent crime or even crime. Strange reports of inexplicable events, suicides, madness and even wild conspiracy theories haunted the estate like a spectre. There had even been reports in the local papers of pets committing suicide by hurling themselves off the high-rise horrors.

The demolition crews had wired the two tower-blocks to blow on the thirty-first of June and demolition went without a hitch. Several days later, the bulldozers had removed the majority of the rubble. It was during the clean-up of the debris in the foundations that the various contractors made a startling discovery which was the reason I was called to the Edwards Estate.

At this point, I was still as much in the dark as to what Winkleman had discovered. His emails had been vague, saying the least. Downright cryptic would more accurate. The man had always harboured a pronounced streak of professional paranoia, so this secrecy didn't come as much of a shock.

At this point, I must confess, I was sorely tempted to tell him to take a walk of the nearest pier. I was still rankled by his going behind my back with the university and I was truly enjoying my home comforts. Still, my professional curiosity was piqued, and I told myself that I should at least humour the old buzzard... How I wish I hadn't...

VI

It was a dismal, rainy Tuesday when I arrived in the car park of Truro University. I hadn't the first idea of where Winkleman might have been hiding so I deemed it prudent to head for the main building and seek out a member of the faculty. The miserable old dragon who was manning reception pointed vaguely towards a distant block and when I turned to head in that direction seemed to take a perverse delight in rudely informing me that, "He's out on a dig, he ain't on campus". When I asked the sour-faced lady where he was, she simply shrugged and went back to the *Times* crossword.

The more I advance in years, the more I

find it increasingly difficult to tolerate rudeness and I was on the verge of giving her a piece of my fuming mind when a helpful student, who had overheard the conversation, diffused the situation with some greatly appreciated information. The young gentleman informed me that Prof. Winkleman and a group of undergraduates had taken equipment and tents to a council estate on the west coast. I thanked the young man and asked him if he knew how to get to the site.

Upon leaving the building and arriving back at my *Land-Rover,* I programmed the information I had been given into the god-forsaken sat-nav device on my dashboard. I endeavour to never use the infernal contraption, but I didn't have an ordinance survey map of the area to hand; sadly. My destination was a fair old drive to the coast, then north through the fishing town of Betyls Cove. Once there, I would try to contact my colleague. And if all else failed I would simply drive around the building site looking for tents.

The journey wasn't an altogether unpleasant one. The sun had eventually poked her head out from behind the clouds and cast beautiful light over the windswept Cornish hillside. The wind was biting, and I was once again glad that I spent what felt like an eternity getting that incompetent garage to finally fix the heater in my vehicle.

By the time I finally reached the outskirts of the Edwards Estate, it had started to get dark. The place was in one hell of a state and it looked as though the builders had simply downed tools and departed. I later found this to be the case. It came as no real surprise that I couldn't manage to reach Winkleman by phone. He was, after all, likely to be down in some subterraneous tunnels.

I had been driving around the accursed Edwards Estate for around half an hour, seemingly in circles, when I finally came across signs of life. Three large green tents, similar to the storm-havens used by the boy scouts, were positioned around a large marquee. Smaller tents and off-road vehicles of varying sizes, emblazoned with the university logo, clustered around the area.

As I drove nearer the dig-site I began noticing activity, there were filthy students with shovels and buckets beavering away around the area. I parked up on the periphery of the camp and stretched my cramping legs, before making my way across the rubble-strewn area. As I neared the marquee, I started to hear the unmistakable dulcet tones of my old friend Professor Winkleman. I entered the marquee, making sure not to disturb anything fragile, and called over at the lumbering figure, that was currently waving a trowel at a startled-looking undergrad. "There you are old chap, I've been looking all over Cornwall for you," I called out across the desolate building site.

"Crabtree, My good man," he boomed in response. "Glad you could join us; we have found such fascinating artefacts... Simply fascinating. Oh, but where are my manners? Team... this is Professor Crabtree from Exeter. He has kindly agreed to lend us his expertise. Crabtree: these are my loyal worker ants. I will do proper introductions over dinner, but for now, you must be knackered from the drive so follow me to the refreshments tent and we'll have a brandy while I fill you in on what's been going on, okay?"

I nodded my agreement, deciding that my admonishment of his meddling could wait, and followed him out of the marquee and over to one of the storm-havens. Tables had been lined up and a makeshift canteen had been erected in the corner. Winkleman directed me to a long wooden decorator's table then splashed a generous helping of brandy into a flimsy plastic cup. Once we had got all of the expected pleasantries out of the way, he proceeded to inform me as to what had recently transpired on the Edwards Estate.

"Alright, dear boy, here's how it started," Winkleman began, "The council had finally decided to rid the world of the two eyesores that made up this god-forsaken housing estate and moved out all the residents out to god knows where. Now, the cowboys that built the wretched things in the first place either didn't notice or didn't care that there was a ruddy great rabbit warren of tunnels under here." He gave his bushy red beard a good stroke before continuing. "The first anyone knew about the tunnels was when a bloody great JCB went crashing through the foundations,"

"Blimey," I interrupted "Was the driver alright?"

"Yeah he was fine," Winkleman waved my

concerns away with a deft flick of his enormous hands. “But, as you can imagine, the whole lot of them basically stuck two fingers up at the council and downed tools. That's why I was initially called in, you know, to do a survey of the area.” Winkleman took a gulp of brandy before refilling our cups and continuing “Now; the town down there,” He waved vaguely south “and pretty much the entirety of Cornwall is littered with bloody holes and tunnels. Whether they be natural or mines or whatever. The town has many tales of smugglers and ne'er-do-wells in the tunnels under here. Heck, they even do tours of them like they do in your neck of the woods.”

He was referring, of course, to the tours of Exeter's winding underground passages.

"Well,” He continued, “those tunnels are well documented and are part of a natural cave system that can be accessed via the sea so are absolutely perfect for smuggling. But nowhere is there a record of the tunnels we are currently investigating. I have scoured the history books, maps and charts but turned up nothing. Also, they appear to be entirely man-made. I'm assuming that there was once a connection to the other tunnels, but it probably caved in at some point, concealing the entrance."

"So, these tunnels, are they smugglers tunnels then?" I asked.

"Well, yes and no. The tunnels are much older. In fact, I'm convinced that they are of Roman construction, judging by tool-marks and carvings. This is why I need your assistance. Nobody I know is better at deciphering Roman carvings and murals than you. But the tunnels were definitely used by the smugglers in the eighteenth-century."

"What makes you so sure?" I asked. "Did you find artefacts?"

Winkleman's face lit up "Artefacts, dear boy? We did better than mere artefacts... We found a bloody battlefield."

***

Over a surprisingly good dinner in the canteen that evening, Winkleman introduced me to his undergrads and continued to inform me about the mysterious tunnels. The JCB that crashed into the tunnel was in the process of clearing debris from the westernmost tower at the time of the incident. Almost directly adjacent to the cave in, Winkleman and his team found a veritable cache of human debris. The bodies had seemingly lain where they had dropped since the day they were cut down.

All the skeletons were complete which was a mystery in and of itself as you would normally expect small furry creatures to have ran off with tasty morsels. They were still dressed in the red coats of the days' soldier or militia. The clothes the skeletons wore were likewise unmolested and no evidence of musket ball holes on either the clothes or remains pointed to an undetermined cause of death. The soldiers had been firing frantically down the westward tunnel, musket-balls and the marks they left on the wall pointed to a somewhat one-sided battle. The muskets lay amongst the bones where they were dropped.

I have to confess that, once again, my interest was piqued. The circumstances of the remarkably well-preserved remains were unusual, to say the least. My initial explanation would point towards a battle between the militia from the east, the most landward point, and smugglers from the sea to the west. But if that was the case then why did the bones and attire show no evidence of musket fire, and I found it ridiculously hard to believe that not one smuggler was killed.

Professor Winkleman's team had fully explored the western tunnel as best they could, but they could only get so far before their progress was impeded by a cave in. Still, even in such short a distance they should have at least found some evidence, no matter how small of the militia's foes. The only reasonable explanation is that the bodies were taken away. But why leave the others? The more I pondered the questions posed by the mysterious tunnels, the more excited I got. I was literally itching to get down there and have a look for myself.

I decided to get a good night's sleep at a local bed and breakfast that Winkleman had kindly booked for me. So after dinner, some healthy banter with the undergrads, and a snifter or two of brandy I called a taxi and turned in for the night. I slept well that night... I haven't slept well since.

VII

Over breakfast the following morning, I studied the photographs of the Roman carvings in great detail. Despite being an expert in the field, I confess to being utterly stumped by the inscriptions. They appeared to conform to no known Latin dialect. I could only surmise that they were some kind of bastardization of the language. If I were to hazard a guess, I would have said that the tunnels were not in fact carved by the Romans but by a people contemporary to the Romans. A people who used the same building method and style of decoration, maybe even a strange sect or society that used their own dialect.

The more I stared at the pictures, the less I learned. For instance, there appeared to be commonly used Latin words that fit with the era. But amongst the recognisable words were ones that I have never encountered before or since. Thus, rendering the whole thing gibberish. I thought that maybe it was some kind of code or cypher.

Whilst I waited for the shuffling zombie that owned the lodgings to bring me my bill, a strange unease settled over me. There was something about the strange words and symbols that sent a chill down my spine. Although, that may have been caused by the freezing sea breeze that whistled from the coast. Despite these feelings, I leapt behind the wheel of my transport, eager for the adventure that lay ahead.

When I arrived at the Edwards Estate, Winkleman was clearly in a heightened state of excitement and was dressed like a nineteenth-century explorer. He was adorned in the very same linen outfit that he had bought on a dig in Egypt back in the nineteen-eighties. Seriously, all the ridiculous man needed was a pith-helmet and a rifle. His students looked similarly eager to get on with the exploration. Many of them carried scientific gizmos of the type that I am convinced will, in time, make people such as myself obsolete.

Winkleman practically pounced on me as I opened the car door. “Morning old chap, I hope you got some rest last night as I can feel that today will be an eventful one.”

“Indeed I did,” I smiled and shook his outstretched hand. “After studying the pictures, you gave me, I'm more intrigued by your mysterious tunnels than I would care to admit.”

“Did you manage to make head or tail of the writing?” He asked, expectantly.

“No, I'm afraid I didn't.” I was reluctantly forced to admit. “It just reads as total gobbledygook to me.”

“Yes,” he replied ruefully. “I feared you would have no more luck with the inscriptions than I. Those damned inscriptions have got the entirety of the British archaeological society scratching their heads. Oh well, let's see if we have better luck elsewhere. The undergrads have been down already and removed the rest of the rubble caused by that bloody digger so it should be safe for us old farts to go down now.

Are you ready, Crabtree?"

“Indeed,” I grinned. Thinking back on my excitement at going down in those dreadful tunnels makes my head spin... If only I could go back and warn us all... “Let's crack on, shall we? Lead the way, old chap.”

With that, I removed my hard hat from the boot of the car and attached the miners light to its clip. I often find it useful to be *hands-free* in these situations. I placed the protective device on my head and donned my utility belt. Once suitably kitted out I joined the assembled team over at the marquee.

I entered and surveyed the scene. I noticed that one of the undergrads, a capable young lady named Sarah, was fussing over a stack of papers. Something was clearly amiss, so I went over to her and asked: “Everything alright there, Sarah?”

“Oh, I'm sure it's nothing really, professor.” She fussed nervously with a stack of sketches. “I just can't seem to find any of the documents relating to the inscriptions anywhere. They have just vanished into thin air.”

“Call me Richard," I smiled, desperately trying to put her at ease. "They must be somewhere, but don't worry, the wall isn't going anywhere. Are you coming down with us today?"

"No, I'm not, prof... err... Richard, a couple of the other students and I are staying put and working on cataloguing the finds from the western tunnel. It suits me really; those tunnels give me the creeps." She shrugged.

She looked slightly embarrassed after her confession so I felt the need to reassure her: "To be honest, the number of human remains you found down there is enough to give anyone the jitters... Myself included." She chuckled at this. I continued. "During the day, why don't you send whichever of your colleagues is irritating you the most down into the tunnel to take more pictures and do more rubbing's and sketches?" This made her grin. "And, if they argue, tell them I put *you* in charge."

At this, Sarah beamed and brushed the mud from her brown hair. "Thank you, Richard, that's a load off my mind, I can just get on with labelling musket-balls now."

I sensed that her joy at labelling musket-balls was insincere but that her gratitude at my advice was entirely truthful. In any case,

I left Sarah looking much brighter and headed over to where Winkleman had just finished instructing his team.

“Ah, Crabtree. All kitted out, are you?” Without waiting for my response, he motioned to the ladder leading down into the hole “Shall we?”

“Indeed,” I said rather too excitedly. "Lay on, Mac-Winkleman” I gestured for him to take the lead.

The undergrads that were joining us on our adventure were already down in the tunnel getting their gear ready. I have always said, you can tell a true archaeologist by their willingness to get up to their elbows in muck and break their backs lugging heavy stones around. By the eager looks on the faces peering up at me, these were true archaeologists.

Winkleman descended the ladder much more nimbly than I would have ever imagined someone of his portly, bear-like stature could achieve. It was my turn next and my creaking knees didn't like that ladder one iota. Still, I think I managed to get down there without looking too decrepit.

Upon reaching the bottom of the tunnel

the first thing that struck me was the rank smell of decay. And when I say struck; I mean like a hammer blow. It was foul by any standard. In fact, it could have rivalled some of the oldest tombs in the world for sheer gag-factor. It was abundantly clear that no fresh air had passed along its length for centuries. It took a good few seconds for me to acclimatise. Once I could again breathe normally, I turned my attention to the tunnel itself.

It had been hand-carved out of the granite and Devonian slate that was typical of the majority of the area's geology. I could only marvel at the effort it must have taken to chip out the surprisingly spacious passage with the primitive tools of the era. From the position and shape of the tunnel, I could tentatively deduce that it was originally a mine of some sort; perhaps one of the oldest in Britain. The area would have been rich in Silver and other precious metals before being bled dry.

Winkleman led the way east along the tunnel. The walls felt damp and the tang of salt on the air hinted at a former connection to the sea; this tied up nicely with the smuggler theory. Winkleman had lost none of his constant bluster in the intervening years since our last encounter and the tunnel echoed with his "Bloody" this and "Bloody" that. It was obvious that his students found this just as amusing as I, as a couple of them were doing a remarkably accurate impression of the bluff old bugger behind me. I shot them both a grin of appreciation.

Not far into our investigation the Tunnel reached a fork. Winkleman split the group into two teams. The northern tunnel graded downwards and was much more cramped. Winkleman sent the two jokers along with a studious-looking girl of German descent down the northern tunnel. Sensibly, he placed the girl, Hedda, in charge. She quickly took charge of her team and led them off down the spur.

Winkleman produced his aerial photograph of the area along with various maps and charts. Using a student's back as a rest, he updated his map with the northern tunnel entrance. Going by the contours shown by a recently conducted GPR survey, and assuming that it stayed true on its trajectory, then the three students would be passing directly under a nearby campsite. Eventually, they would end up down near the lighthouse to the north. Our tunnel would continue east towards the site of the second tower-block.

Winkleman explained that the GPR didn't turn up the tunnels as, at the time of the survey, tons of humanity and concrete stood on the main site and that the northern contours were explained originally as natural pot-holes or caverns. This would have been perfectly plausible as Cornwall is riddled like Swiss cheese with such features.

We made quick progress. Beyond the cave-in, the tunnel was relatively free from debris. We found several fragments of Roman pottery which we duly bagged and tagged. Though, I have to confess, when you have experienced as many digs as I have it's hard to become overly excited by fragments of ancient crockery.

We had reached the halfway point when the deafening echo of stomping feet alerted us to the presence of one of the students we sent north. The breathless undergrad with the almost impenetrable Cornish accent, that had earlier been mocking my esteemed colleague, informed us that they had reached a point where the tunnel had been deliberately collapsed by blasting. He marked the break on Winkleman's map and returned to his fellows with the instruction to return to the surface with anything of interest. Winkleman was obviously disappointed by the news but reflected optimistically that it meant we could put all of our eggs in one basket, so to speak.

After a short while, it seemed as though our investigation was to be similarly thwarted. Just before our intended destination, we ran into another cave-in that was definitely caused by deliberate human action. The tell-tale marks, chips and fragments of blasting spoke volumes.

Luckily for us, It appeared that the effort had not been entirely successful. Using a pen light, I peered through gaps in the rubble. The tunnel continued on its course after the obstruction. Winkleman instructed his team to retrieve the wheelbarrows and some metal supports from camp. Then gather a team and get the rubble shifted. For now, they could dump said rubble in the useless northern tunnel. He then proposed that we get out from under their feet, break for lunch and examine the pottery and anything the northern team found.

This sounded like a good plan to me as my stomach had started rumbling. Plus, with my back, I would have been less than useless in the excavation party. We made our way back down the tunnel and ascended the ladder.

VIII

Winkleman, and others, had often mocked my obsessive planning despite it always paying dividends and, happily, I had remembered my prescription sunglasses. I replaced my spectacles, so I wasn't completely blinded by the bright sun when I emerged from the tunnel. Unlike my bumbling companion, who proceeded to stumble around like a drunken walrus.

As I exited the marquee, I was greeted by a highly agitated Sarah. The poor girl looked as though her nerves were well and truly frayed. She was chewing her nails down to the quick and proceeded to babble at me about a highly odd event. “Richard,” she called out hysterically and dragged me off to one side by the elbow. “Something weird has happened and I don't know if I'm going mad or what... Winkleman is going to blow a fuse.”

“Hold on, calm down... Just breathe.” I tried my best to bring her off the boil and down to a gentle simmer. “Start from the beginning. What's happened?”

She took a deep breath and held it to the count of ten then began. “I sent Adam down to take pictures as we discussed, but he came back looking confused. Professor Crabtree... The inscriptions have gone.”

I admit that I looked at the poor girl like she had just beamed down from Pluto. “Gone? What do you mean, *gone*? Has there been a cave-in?”

“Just gone,” she exclaimed. “The wall is still intact but there is nothing there, not a scratch.”

As you would imagine, I feared a mistake or a student prank, so I descended, with Sarah in tow, to examine the wall. “And you're sure this is the place?” I asked when we reached the spot she indicated.

"Completely." She stated emphatically. "I was on the team that took the original pictures, it was right here." Sarah was visibly shaken by this strange turn of events, so I sent her topside and elected to inform Winkleman myself in an effort to save her his inevitably rigorous, and likely offensive, cross-examination. He didn't cope with stress very well... Another gross understatement.

As I fully expected, Winkleman blew his top when I told him of the development, and he went racing off down the tunnel like a shot. I had never seen the man move so quickly, except when last-orders were called in the local pub. After an agonizing few minutes, during which the students made themselves scarce, he returned. His face looked like a particularly grumpy beetroot and he was angrily muttering to himself about it being "Bloody Impossible."

Winkleman went charging off towards the tent where Sarah and the others were dutifully bagging pottery. I couldn't hear what was being said, but judging by the frantic waving of his arms, I guessed that Sarah had informed him about the missing pictures and that he was deeply unhappy about the fact. Sarah giving him the middle finger as he walked away practically confirmed my suspicions.

As my colleague tore through the camp like a tornado, I soon remembered the facsimiles that Winkleman had provided me with the night before. Ignoring the commotion, I walked to my *Land Rover* and checked the glovebox... They were still there. I thanked the Lord and called Winkleman over as I wanted to tell him in confidence about the file. I deemed a certain level of secrecy prudent as we didn't know the circumstances of the data's disappearance. Winkleman breathed a sigh of relief and turned a lighter shade of red, which was reassuring as his blood-pressure must have been sky-high at that point. He was lucky he hadn't dropped dead of a heart attack. After secreting the documents under the carpet in the boot, we decided to grab a bite to eat and have a fortifying brandy before the rigours of the afternoon began.

I consumed a hearty ham and cheese ploughman's while my colleague ranted and raved about conspiracies of rival teams trying to scupper his findings. After a while, however, he calmed down and his enthusiasm for the second tower site returned with aplomb.

After a while, it struck me as decidedly odd that neither of us had heard anything from the tunnel diggers nor the northern clearance team, so we decided to head back down to the tunnels. As we reached the place where the students were supposed to be clearing rubble, it became clear that we were alone. Shovels and wheelbarrows lay abandoned and the tunnel had been completely cleared of debris.

Winkleman didn't seem at all concerned by his missing team and figured that they must have simply broken for lunch. I, however, wasn't so sure. Leaving him to poke around in the dust, I returned to the fork in the tunnel and headed north. It wasn't long before I reached the designated dumping ground for the rubble. The bizarre thing was that the students had piled the rubble high, blocking the north tunnel completely.

Winkleman had advanced down the tunnel and was bellowing my name with a fervour I wouldn't have credited him for. I attempted to inform him about the newly constructed wall and urge him to return topside to look for his team but he waved my concerns aside and put it down to, "Bloody students, playing a bloody prank then buggering off to the pub." His blasé attitude to this kind of thing had always irritated me but I knew that when he was in this kind of mood there was no reasoning with him.

I held my tongue and followed him along the tunnel. Soon, the cause of his excitement became readily apparent. we were directly below where the second tower-block had stood and, before us, the tunnel ended in a wall of eighteenth-century construction. He told me to fetch a sledgehammer from where his students had left one. This I did with all due haste... I was chomping at the bit to see what lay beyond.

The ancient stone quickly yielded under the force of Winkleman's expertly swung sledgehammer. A rush of musty feted air assaulted our senses and caused us both to choke and splutter. I hurriedly placed a handkerchief over my nose and mouth and Winkleman did the same. We waited for the dust to settle before continuing on.

The tunnel opened onto a large room with a high vaulted ceiling. When visibility cleared sufficiently, it became apparent that we were in some sort of cellar.

"The Edwards Estate," Winkleman barked

excitedly. When I asked him what the devil he was banging on about, he continued. "This must be part of the original Edwards Estate. The housing development was named after the land's former life as the grounds to Edwards Manor. You see, old chap, the land was owned by a wealthy family called Edwards. The final owner of the estate was a corrupt squire with links to smuggling and all kinds of roguish activities. The man was a complete scoundrel by all accounts and was believed to have perished when the manor burned down. The entire property was believed to have been erased but it looks like those cowboys in the sixties did a poor job of it. Thank Christ for those idiots, If it wasn't for their corner-cutting then what we now standing in would be a bloody great slab of concrete."

"So, this is the manor cellar?" I clarified.

"Indeed... Perfectly preserved under tons of concrete and glass... You know, it's a testament to the solidity of the foundations that the whole thing didn't collapse in upon itself." As he was talking, Winkleman had started poking around the spacious interior. The room was packed with interesting artefacts, there was even a modest collection of undoubtedly priceless bottles of wine. There were boxes of documents, antiques and keepsakes. There were things here that museums and private collectors across the globe would gleefully sell their mothers for.

A sharp cry of "Bugger me backwards," alerted me that Winkleman had made some kind of discovery. I hastened across to where he was standing and was startled by what I saw. In a high-backed and ornately carven wooden chair, complete with gold-trim and various decorative embellishments, sat the skeleton of a man.

The skeleton was adorned in a fancy frockcoat, a long wig similar to that of a judge and a tricorn hat. It didn't take much guesswork to deduce that before us, sat the earthly remains of Squire Edwards. Before him on a stout desk sat a goblet, an ink well, a quill, various sheets of high-quality parchment and a bizarrely carven scrimshaw or sailor's charm.

Winkleman was extolling the unique nature of the scrimshaw. It was indeed a fascinating object. it appeared to have been carved from whalebone and seemed to depict a large sea-monster or Kraken. The totem was similar to others that I have seen originating in the south seas. What set this piece apart was the strange inscriptions around the base, they seemed to use a strange dialect unknown to both myself and my colleague, the same strange language as the wall carving that had just recently inexplicably vanished.

Winkleman tucked the scrimshaw into his pocket and continued to explore. Meanwhile, I had begun to cast my eyes over the scribblings of the dead squire. It was clear from just a glance that the man had completely lost his marbles, and by the end was as mad as a March-hare. Most of his voluminous notes spoke of a curse. Some sort of devil's bargain that he and a smuggler cohort called Tremayne had made which was bringing doom to the entire region. Amongst the deluded ramblings and insane ravings, I managed to piece together a narrative of the events directly leading to his demise.

According to Squire Edwards' notes, the port had been besieged by an unidentified force that he called Deep Ones. He described this force as being gill breathing men and women that lived in various underwater cities. He went on to explain that they were at that moment closing in on him and his men. Something had irked these Deep Ones, something about his reneging on a bargain, now they came for their pound of flesh.

In an attempt to halt the advance of the assault, that appeared to have taken place entirely in these very tunnels, Squire Edwards had his men rig the tunnels with gunpowder. As his men fought valiantly against their aquatic foes, the duplicitous Squire lit the fuses. Entombing both his attackers and his men. This explained the bodies that Winkleman had discovered. The poor devils must have starved to death.

Well pleased with his despicable work, the squire set about sealing up his cellar with the help of some of his smuggling chums as though there had never been any tunnels. But he too had been betrayed. After the tunnel had been blocked, he retired to bed. Then the following morning he returned to the cellar to destroy any evidence of his activities and to get rid of a certain trinket. While the Squire was destroying evidence, the same sailors that had helped him seal the tunnel shut the cellar hatch, weighted it down with rocks and torched the manor. It is unknown how long the Squire was entombed before he gave in and poisoned himself with arsenic, one of the abundant local metals, but it looked to me, at that time, that he had gone completely mad... If only that had been the case.

The remainder of the notes spoke of a formless horror lurking in the sealed passages. The tormented man was convinced that the deep ones had unleashed something he called a *shoggoth* into the subterraneous network via one of the sea caves. Possibly the one at the Blasted Crag. He was tormented by nightmares and delusions. Hearing noises behind the tapestry, there was indeed a tapestry on the western wall that dated back to when the cellar was a Roman temple of some sort, he turned to certain mystical tomes that he had inherited from his *wizard* grandfather.

Edwards' family line stretched all the way back to the founding of the town and still continues today. In fact, one of the young chaps from the dig, the one with the thick accent, was a local Edwards; though something of a black sheep. Amongst their vast heritage, they had amongst their number more than one who dabbled in certain *black* arts.

Using something he called an *Elder sign;* Edwards sealed the passages and was seemingly able to keep whatever was lurking at bay. Not that this helped him any. He was still trapped under the smouldering wreckage of his home with only a few dozen bottles of wine for sustenance. He had tried to hold out for as long as possible but when it became abundantly clear that no help was coming, he set about writing the very document I held in my hands... His suicide note.

He concluded his rambling testimony by warning whoever may come across his remains about the danger of the scrimshaw. It was this object that the shoggoth was after. Apparently, it held some sort of control over the unspeakable beast. Edwards had tried to destroy it many times to no avail. It was this trinket, according to Edwards, that bound him to his bargain and wouldn't let him go. This was the very trinket that now resided in Winkleman's coat pocket.

I had been reading the salient points to my companion and upon reading the passage about the tapestry, Winkleman moved some boxes out of the way and started to examine the dusty relic. It was a vile object depicting a horrific scene of slaughter and mayhem in the worship of some strange cephalopod-headed deity. I vaguely recalled seeing drawings of a similar nature in the *forbidden* books that my undergraduate chums and I had stolen a look at in the Cambridge University library.

Whilst Winkleman fiddled with the monstrous tapestry, I moved over to where we had broken our way into the cellar. Amongst the pile of bricks and dust, was a stone tablet that was now cleaved in two. Picking up the two halves and putting them together, it became clear that this was one of the seals that Edwards had been talking about. It had been attached to the wall with metal spikes and depicted a five-pointed star with a strange flame-like design in the centre. The sign was completed with more of the strange writing under the star.

While I had been examining the strange seal, Winkleman had been methodically unfastening the tapestry from the wall. If it was as old as it appeared, then this unnerving decoration could be the jewel in Winkleman's crown. As it fell away, it revealed something we hadn't at all expected... A door.

“Bloody hell,” Winkleman exclaimed. The stout wooden door was barred with a series of bolts and in the centre, attached with chains, was another seal. I crossed the room and joined him. He was already in the process of removing the seal.

“Careful with that." I chided him. For all I knew, there were only two of the strange seals still in existence. "The other one is in two lumps thanks to your sledgehammer."

Winkleman harrumphed and gently completed his task. Once the seal was removed, he passed it to me. “Careful with that.” He grinned.

“Touché,” I replied and set it gently down on the squire's desk.

Winkleman shot the bolts and pulled the ancient, creaking door open using a large metal ring. The stench that billowed forth from the aperture made everything else I had smelt that day pale in comparison. It reeked of rotten fish and decay. I gagged and reached once again for my trusty handkerchief.

Now, I think it is fair to say that Anybody

who knows me can attest that I am not a nervous or anxious person... Far from it. Nor am I usually given to flights of fancy. But after reading the Squires notes, along with the disappearing inscription, the disappearing undergrads and the evidence of a pitched battle, I was convinced that entering the newly discovered tunnel would bring us nought but peril. The lightless passage was foreboding to say the very least.

Unfortunately, my obstinate friend didn't feel the same. He was so excited by the possibility of an area untrodden for centuries that before I could say: "Don't go down there you fool," he was charging through the doorway, torch in hand.

Cautiously, I followed him inside. The floor was slick with slime and filth making it treacherous and the walls were of a furred appearance due to the prodigious growth of moss and lichens. The atmosphere was stifling, and a pronounced feeling of dread overtook my rational thoughts, I was convinced that there was something in that vile space with us. It didn't help that every noise echoed and reverberated off the tightly enclosed walls. It seemed that

I was not the only one feeling discomfort as Winkleman's reassuring grumblings had gone strangely quiet.

We had been heading on a downward gradient for what I estimated to be around half a mile when Winkleman suddenly stopped in his tracks. Every muscle in his body had tensed and it appeared as though all his hair was on end like a huge ginger cat upon coming face to face with a dog. “Did you hear that?” He hissed.

“No, what did you hear?” I responded and as I spoke, I too became frozen in fear. From somewhere ahead came a strange gurgling sound that I struggle to describe in any way that would do it justice, other than to say, that it sounded how I imagine a gallon of jelly and gravel being sucked down a plug-hole to sound.

As we stood paralysed with fear, the strange slurping sound was joined by a chillingly strange noise, a kind of shrill manic buzz, like an angry wasp stuck in a flute. Worse, the noise was getting steadily louder with every passing moment, it sounded as though something enormous was hurtling towards us.

Almost as if we were both in the same

mind, Winkleman and I turned on our heels and began to slip and slide back up the tunnel for our lives. The noise was becoming deafening and an unholy foul stench seemed to build with every passing moment. Whatever ghastly terror was on heels, it was certainly quick. The high-pitched warble it emanated seemed to gather in intensity the closer it got to its prey... Us.

My friend and I made surprisingly quick progress back through the tunnel puffing and wheezing like a couple of old dray-horses. The unspeakable *thing* was almost upon us by the time we neared the cellar entrance and we scrambled with all our remaining strength and ran straight into the barrel of an old service revolver.

Standing in the entrance waving an antique flintlock pistol was Henry Edwards, the previously mocking student. The pistol was levelled right between my eyes "Give me the fuckin' scrimshaw or I'll shoot," he barked in his thick Cornish burr. The thing in the tunnel was closing in and I was sure of my impending demise, either from *it* or a well-placed bullet, when suddenly, Winkleman saved the day.

For once, Professor Winkleman's bullish

ways proved a great help, not a hindrance. "Out of my way you bloody idiot," he bellowed and barged Henry out of our path without any thought of being shot. Henry's head cracked the wall and he dropped the pistol. The force of my brutish friend sent him tumbling to the slimy sloping floor and he began to slide head-first towards the slurping menace.

Winkleman and I made it to the cellar and managed to close and lock the door just as a blood-curdling scream echoed around the chamber accompanied by a slurping, sucking noise. It was as though whatever had been stalking us was now sucking Henry's bones clean... We paused to catch our breath, amazed that we had managed to outrun the terrible *thing* in the tunnel.

Suddenly, the trilling noise started again, and I was horrified by what I saw. From the gaps around the door seeped an iridescent black ooze that seemed to be reforming into a growing globular mass. If I hadn't already lost all of my hair save a few grey patches around the back, then I'm sure it would have turned white. There were eyes in the ooze, hundreds of eyes, popping in and out of the formless terror.

"Quick," I screamed. "The seal,"

Winkleman bounded across the cellar and grabbed the seal. As he advanced on the door, the creature shrieked in terror and recoiled. It went back into the tunnel and I could clearly hear it retreating. The next few minutes were a blur as we made sure that the seal was back in place. We hastened from the cellar and headed topside.

IX

Upon leaving the marquee, a scene of utter devastation greeted us. All the technological equipment had been smashed and everything else had either also been smashed or burned. The site looked like a bombsite and there were casualties to boot. The bodies of two students, Adam and a promising young chap called Ben were laying outside the canteen tent with their skulls caved in. Inside the canteen lay Sarah with a similar blow to the head but thank the Lord, she was still alive. She was barely conscious and obviously concussed.

She was slightly delirious but managed to tell us that it was Henry who caused this carnage and that he was looking for the scrimshaw. When he couldn't find it he became violent and attacked the three students with a strange ferocity then left them for dead.

Winkleman tenderly gathered Sarah in his tree-trunk arms and placed her in my Land-Rover. Together we drove her to the hospital where she thankfully made a full recovery. She had a concussion, as I expected, but aside from that, she was fine.

While we sat outside the A&E Winkleman and I had a heated discussion which I'm glad to say I won for once. I managed to convince Winkleman that the best thing to do was photograph the scrimshaw then throw it back into the sea where it belongs. It was clearly a harbinger of doom and horror and by returning it to the sea I hoped that the shoggoth would leave Betyls Cove and go back to whence it came.

The three of us stayed at Truro University while the local police investigated the murders. The men in charge, DI Baker and DS Finch interviewed us on more than a few occasions. We had decided to leave out the part about the monstrous shoggoth from our narrative. We had told Sarah what had happened below but swore her to secrecy.

It was obvious that the police had discovered more than they let on, but we never spoke of it. I initially took charge of the scrimshaw, intending to dispose of it when I was allowed to leave campus. Every night, I was assailed by the most horrific nightmares of a city under the sea. It was populated by hideous hybrid creatures that worshipped the squid-god-thing. It seemed to hold a strange fascination for me. I even found myself plotting to keep it for myself.

In the end, we entrusted the disposal of the scrimshaw to Sarah, as she was the one amongst us least affected by its insidious allure. She vowed to toss it off the Blasted Crag when she returned home to Betyls Cove. I only hope that she did.

Winkleman and I continued to investigate the events in total secrecy and have since turned up some interesting facts: The majority of instances of violent crime, murders, rapes, etc. were committed in and around the first tower where the battle between that *thing* and the militia had taken place. Secondly, the second tower was the scene of the bulk of reports pertaining to suicides and madness, just like Squire Edwards. I can only surmise that the residual psychic residue was somehow amplified by the unholy scrimshaw.

The facsimile pictures that Winkleman provided me with are still in my care, nobody except he and I know of their existence. On my travels a year later, I came across a number of star-shaped stones in a strange temple in Peru. They were undoubtedly the Elder sign. I have enclosed one in the envelope that I will place this document into upon completion.

This brings me neatly to the end of my narrative. I have compiled this document as I was recently contacted by Sarah. She informed me that she was currently living in one of the newly built flats directly over the site of the cellar. She has seemingly taken it upon herself to become a self-appointed guardian of the secrets under the town. I felt it was necessary to have all the facts to aid her in her noble quest, so I am sending her this document along with the copies of the inscriptions and other documents... To be honest, I'm grateful to be finally getting rid of them.

I end this now with a solemn hope that is going to sound strange coming from an archaeologist, but I am glad the tunnels are seemingly blocked off and I hope this continues to be the case... Some things are just best left buried.

PART 3

The Thing From Below

X

PC Granger turned the scrimshaw over in her hands as Sergeant Fisher finished reading aloud Professor Crabtree's disturbing testimony. Sarah had left the scrimshaw resting on what turned out to be *her* suicide note. She blamed herself for what was happening. She never did dispose of the scrimshaw. She wasn't as immune to its charms as Crabtree had thought. It was for this item, Sarah had written, that the shoggoth had returned. Therefore, in her troubled mind, this was all her stupid fault.

Fisher closed the book and pinched the bridge of his bulbous nose with his thumb and forefinger. “Bloody hell.” He muttered under his breath. Under normal circumstances he would have shrugged Crabtree's account off as the ravings of a potty old academic, but these were far from normal circumstances. “Now what?” He looked pleadingly at the others for just a spark of an idea.

“Can't we just give the shoggoth what it wants?” Paul asked. “The scrimshaw, I mean.”

“Then what?” Fisher replied.

“Then it might just, you know, leave.”

“Have you seen that thing?” Fisher asked rhetorically. “I don't think that its the type of thing you can bargain with. At the moment, it's stuck here... Contained. If we give it the scrimshaw, it will be free to go where it likes... Shit... Imagine that thing loose in the town...”

Paul shuddered.

“We need to seal it back up.” Granger put the scrimshaw on the desk and picked up the strange star-headed talisman. “The builders must have disturbed the seal. That means that the cellar must still be under here... Bloody cowboys... It should have been flooded with concrete... Then we wouldn't be in this mess.

Kyle walked over to the desk and picked up the scrimshaw. Holding it up to the light, he gazed at the strange writing. He didn't believe half of the things he had heard and was sure that there was another explanation... A failed government experiment, perhaps. He chose to keep his mouth shut at this point, fearing the wrath of the group. Still, the scrimshaw *was* weird, that's for sure.

"How the hell would we get down there?" Paul was looking out of the window at his van. He would have given anything at that point to just get in and drive to the pub. "*Can* we even get down there?"

"According to Sarah, yes." Fisher had found a number of plans of the building that Sarah must have acquired from the town hall. She had drawn on them in red-felt tip. It looked like there was a way down through the maintenance tunnels in the basement level. "She had been doing some research. There seems to be a way in through here..." She held the map under Fisher's nose and jabbed at the point with her finger. "Problem is... We need a special key for the maintenance door in order to access the lower level. She says that the caretaker had one."

"That'd be Jim York." Paul nodded. "You

know... Old geezer that used to work on the fishing boats; always pissed out of his skull on the benches outside the Freemason's?"

Fisher nodded. "Yeah, I know him. Did him for petty theft back in the day."

"Well, he lives on the ground floor. I had to fit a new tap for him a while back. He got the flat as part of the job. He's supposed to be on call twenty-four seven..."

"Yeah... Right." Fisher snorted derisively. "The only thing he's on call for is last orders. Still, he should be in... Unless..." While they had been reading Crabtree's account, screams and the sounds of destruction had echoed from the floors below. If Jim was indeed home, then his chances of survival were slim.

"Damn." Paul huffed. "Looks like we will have to go into his flat and get the key."

As the others nodded, Kyle exploded. "We? What's all this *we* business. I'm not going anywhere,"

"Come on, Kyle. *We* are all in this mess together... Aren't we?" At this, Kyle snorted once again. Paul snapped. "Don't be a useless tosser all your life."

"Screw you. If you want to go and get

killed by that thing... Fine. Just don't expect me to follow you. I'm going to sit tight and wait for rescue." Kyle stormed into the kitchen and slammed the door behind him.

Paul gritted his teeth and growled. Clenching and unclenching his fists, he counted to ten and tried to get his rage in check. "What a wanker," he finally blurted, a sentiment that got an appreciative nod from Granger. "Who the fuck does he think is coming? The bloody *A-Team*?"

"Calm down, Paul." Granger said softly. "Don't worry about him. We shall see how much he wants to stay here once we break Sarah's wards when we open the door."

A smirk passed over Paul's lips and he visibly relaxed. "I'll go and check on the bathroom." He announced, picking up his bag of salt and leaving the room.

"You're good at handling those two." Fisher said as he studied the building plan. "I'd have just banged their ruddy heads together."

Fisher rarely doled out praise, Granger blushed despite herself. "So, what's the plan then, Sarge?"

Fisher stroked his chin thoughtfully for

a second. “We go down to the ground floor and get the maintenance key from Jim's flat. Then, we find a way into the tunnels. Lure the shoggoth down there and seal it up somehow...”

“As easy as that, huh?” Granger smiled. “How do we lure it down there? I for one am not keen on offering myself up as a tasty snack.”

“The scrimshaw.” Fisher said matter-of-factly. “It wants the scrimshaw, so we throw it down the tunnel and slam the door behind it... Hold on... Where is the scrimshaw?”

A moment of panic gripped Granger's soul as she frantically looked under the desk for the missing totem.

“Bathroom's fine for now.” Paul announced upon his return. He looked at Fisher and Granger who were both searching for something. “What have you lost?”

“The sodding scrimshaw,” Fisher boomed in response.

“Kyle had it.” Paul shrugged. “It was in his hand when he stormed off. He'd been staring at it for ages.”

Fisher looked at Granger and swallowed. Something about this didn't feel right. His finely attuned 'coppers sixth sense' tingled and he stood up sharply. “I'm going to get it back. Come with me, Charlotte. He seems to listen to you.”

Granger nodded and followed her superior to the kitchen. She paused and listened at the door. Kyle was muttering to himself about something. Gently, she knocked on the door with the middle knuckle of her bent forefinger. “Kyle? Is everything okay in there?”

“Yes. Everything is fine... Go away,” Kyle sounded hysterical.

“Okay, Kyle.” Granger said calmly. “We need the scrimshaw. Can you pass it to me?”

Kyle didn't answer but Granger could hear him talking quietly. She couldn't make out what he was saying, but it sounded like he was cooing at something... Like you do to a kitten.

“I think he's talking down the plug-hole.” Granger whispered.

Fisher straightened up to his full height and clenched his fists. “I've had quite enough of this.” He banged on the door like it was a drug bust. “I'm coming in. Hand over the blasted scrimshaw.”

“No,” Kyle screamed in reply. “You can't

have it. It's mine."

Fisher had heard enough. "Sod this," he growled as he yanked the door open.

There was a collective gasp from the three. "What the hell are you doing?" Paul demanded.

Kyle was holding the scrimshaw in his cupped hands over the sink. He was completely oblivious to their entry; he was mesmerized by what was coming out of the sink.

"Holy shit," Fisher barked.

The shoggoth had come up from the drain and had filled the sink. It bulged upwards towards the scrimshaw. Hundreds of orange eyes all gazed up at the object, seemingly in reverence. "That's it... Good boy." Kyle muttered.

"Kyle," Granger screamed.

His head snapped around. He had a dopey grin on his face and his eyes burned with the same orange of the shoggoth's.

"Give me the scrimshaw," she said firmly but calmly.

Kyle shook his head. "No... It's mine."

"Hand it over," Fisher grunted. "I'll take it by force if necessary."

Kyle grinned wider. "It's mine... The

shoggoth... It's mine to control." His face took on a harder, menacing aspect as his eyes sharpened like needles. "Stay back."

"One last time..." Fisher took out his police baton and flicked it to its full extension. "Give me the blasted scrimshaw... Now."

Kyle jerked mechanically and started to chant. The words ululated and hung in the air like a miasma. The shoggoth started to stretch from the sink. A massive tentacle shot up into the air and awaited Kyle's instruction. "Shoggoth..." Kyle giggled. "Kill."

The tentacle reared back and prepared to strike. Fisher acted quickly and swung the baton. It connected with Kyle's elbow. The shock along his ulnar nerve was anything but funny and caused his arm to spasm. The scrimshaw rocketed into the air and clattered off the light-fitting.

"No," Kyle screamed in rage and dismay as the tentacle, free of his control, turned its attention to him. It surged forwards and coiled like a serpent around his wrist.

Paul deftly caught the scrimshaw and stashed it in his utility belt. "Out."

Fisher and Granger followed his lead.

Granger thought to try and save Kyle, but it was already too late. The tip of the tentacle pierced his wrist and flooded his arteries. His mouth opened in a bellow of rage as his eyes burst and were replaced by shimmering black orbs.

"Tekeli-li," Kyle growled. Though it came from his vocal cords, the voice most certainly wasn't kyle's. His free arm jerked towards Granger. The skin rippled and burst. Hundreds of miniscule eyes appeared on his ruined flesh like daemonic frogspawn. "Tekeli-li."

Granger slammed the door and followed Paul and Fisher out of the flat and into the corridor leaving Kyle to lie in the bed he had made for himself. The pangs of guilt were quickly destroyed by the adrenaline of escape.

The roof had been ripped open and the chill Cornish rain lashed down onto their heads. The rampaging shoggoth had done a lot of damage. The walls had buckled and cracked. Doors had been smashed and the overpowering stench of freshly squeezed blood drifted on the harsh wind. The worst of the damage, however, had been reserved for the floor. About halfway along the corridor, just before the stairs, was a massive hole about three meters across.

"Now what?" Paul despaired. There wasn't a way in hell that he and Fisher could jump it. Granger wouldn't have a problem but neither man was in what you could describe as tip-top condition.

Finch peered over the edge and looked down at the floor below. As luck would have it, it seemed to be intact. "Let's drop down... I'll go first and catch you."

Paul nodded. It made sense and the ceiling wasn't exactly high. It only meant dropping about a foot. Knelt down then swung his legs over. Granger held on to his shoulder to steady him. Once he was in position, he dangled himself fully then let go. He landed safely and steadied himself on the wall.

Granger went next. She nimbly jumped through the hole and landed like a cat. Next, it was Paul's turn and he didn't like heights. Just peering down gave him a sense of vertigo.

"Just lower yourself." Fisher instructed. "We will lower you down."

Paul gulped and moved himself into position. He screwed his eyes up tightly, held his breath and let his legs dangle. The feeling of

Fisher grabbing his work-boot was a welcome one and as he and Granger grabbed his legs, he was able to breathe once again.

Tekeli-li

With an almighty crash, the door to Sarah's flat exploded in a shower of splinters as the seething mass of hateful protoplasm burst out into the corridor. Paul's eyes opened and he saw to his horror that the hide of the creature wore a grotesquely distorted parody of Kyle's face. “Tekeli-li,” the dreadful call of the shoggoth boomed out of its warped grin as it hurtled down the corridor.

Paul screamed and lunged backwards. He plunged through the hole, bottom first, and bowled Fisher and Granger over. They landed on their backs in a heap just below the hole.

The shoggoth loomed above them. Its evil eyes dancing with hunger. Kyle's face stretched and twisted; the mouth moving mechanically. “Tekeli-li.” Several tendrils sprouted from its body and started to snake down the hole. They dangled just inches from Granger's face.

“Back, you bastard,” Fisher growled and lobbed one of the bags of salt that he had pocketed at the creature. It burst in a white cloud that not only sent the creature reeling but also temporarily blinded PC Granger. Both she and the shoggoth cried out in pain.

Paul was to his feet first. He grabbed Granger under the arms and hauled her to her feet. Fisher gave them a head start then lobbed a second open bag of salt at the shoggoth. This one hit the bullseye. Kyle's face bubbled and ran, streaking down the shoggoth's bulk as it trembled and howled. While the shoggoth was stunned, Fisher ran like he was a teenager again.

“Quick, down the stairs,” Fisher screamed as he caught up with the others.

Paul grabbed Granger by the hand and helped to guide her into the staircase. Tears were streaming down her face as she tried to blink the salt from them. Once on the stairs she grabbed hold of the rail and used it to guide herself.

The three survivors raced down the stairs as fast as they could. Above, the shoggoth screamed and howled. It wasn't long before they had reached the ground floor. They were safe... For the moment.

XI

Jim York shivered in the torrential downpour that had broken out over Betyls Cove. The sixty-something caretaker with a taste for the booze and an eye for the ladies felt like a freshly reheated cadaver. He hadn't made it home after the previous night's session and had passed out on a bench in the graveyard. His head had been pounding ever since he was rudely awakened by the verger half an hour earlier.

Removing the electronic door fob from his back pocket, Jim stared at the door in incomprehension. The damn thing wouldn't open. He punched in the override code only to receive the same disappointing results. It was then that he noticed that the power to the door had been shut off. The lack of LED lights and digital display was a bit of a giveaway that he should have spotted sooner. Cursing under his breath, Jim rifled through his pockets in an attempt to find the good-old-fashioned Yale key that would open the door.

As he fished in the lining of his coat, he spotted something out of the corner of his eye. Lying broken and motionless just along the side of the building was the body of one of the tenants, Sarah. Jim gingerly approached the corpse. He didn't need to check for a pulse. She was definitely dead. The sight of her split skull made him heave. Rushing over to the grid next to the door, Jim violently purged the last night's alcohol from his guts.

This was when he spotted all that remained of poor Sid. Around the drain was a sticky substance that contained clumps of bristly hair, fingernails and half a melted trainer. Jim's vision swam as he turned sharply away from the foul substance. His legs wobbled and he had to grab hold of a lamppost to stop himself hurtling face-first into the flagstones.

Once his equilibrium stabilised, Jim pulled

out his mobile phone and swore. The battery was flat. Not that he ever had a signal anyway. He gathered his thoughts and hurried down the path and in the direction of the phone-box on the corner...

***

DS Finch got that sinking feeling that veteran copper's get when they hear certain calls. He had been quite happily munching a bacon sandwich when his radio squawked. When he heard the words “Dead Body,” “Strange goo,” and “Burridge Court,” He knew deep down what it meant. As one of the investigating officers on the case of the 'Edwards Estate dig massacre' he knew only too well what was reportedly lurking under the town.

Along with DI Baker, Finch had been one of the first on the scene. Professor Winkleman had told him what happened, and though it sounded insane, he knew it to be true. His suspicions were all but confirmed later that evening when the army and some government suits appeared waving the official secrets act under everyone's nose. They had investigated as best as they could, but the official red tape bound their hands tightly behind their backs. They weren't even allowed down into the tunnels to search for the bodies of the missing students.

All these memories came flooding back as he accepted the shout to go to Burridge Court and investigate. He brushed the crumbs off his drooping moustache and stormed out of the canteen. Approaching the doors, he spotted his old friend PC Alice Fielding.

"Alice." He grunted. "I need you to come with me to Burridge Court. We got a stiff on the lawn. Looks like a suicide.

Fielding nodded and took her keys from the desk.

Finch barked at some other loitering constables and told them to meet them there. Something told him that he was going to need backup.

***

Jim sucked thirstily at the half-bottle of Scotch whiskey that he had just bought from the nearby off license as he waited for the police to arrive. The fiery spirit had banished his hangover in one mighty gulp, and he was feeling vaguely human again. It was no small wonder that they called it the water of life.

Replacing the screwcap, he slipped the bottle into the inside pocket of his filthy raincoat as a marked police vehicle pulled into the car park. Lighting a roll-up, Jim walked over and Greeted DS Finch as he hauled his huge frame from the passenger seat. “Morning, Billy. Lovely day for it.” He looked up at the glowering skies and pouring rain and grimaced.

“Jim.” Finch nodded. “Been on the sauce already?” He sniffed the pungent aroma of distilled alcohol on the dishevelled caretaker's breath.

“You're going to need a nip when you see what I have seen.” Jim replied without a hint of humour. “Bloody horrible sight. I think it's Crazy Sarah. You know, the one from *the dig*?”

This revelation added to DS Finch's unease. Yes, he knew Sarah alright. He had personally taken the shaken and concussed young student's statement after the horrors of the archaeological dig. “Shite,” He whispered to himself. “Okay, Jim. Lead on.”

The two men and PC Fielding trudged

across the waterlogged lawn at the front of the building. Two constables were already at the body and were looking decidedly green around the gills. Finch stood over Sarah's body and looked up at her balcony. It was obvious that she had either jumped or was pushed as there was a high wall preventing a slip or fall.

As he looked up at the side of the block, he spotted something odd. The wall adjacent to Sarah's flat seemed to bulge outwards as though something huge had slammed into it. A large chunk of cladding had fallen off the side of the building and had smashed into fragments on the walkway below.

"Damn." Finch muttered under his breath. "Bloody builders must have disturbed it."

"What was that, Sarge?" Fielding asked, her neat brown eyebrow arched and her eyes questioning.

"Oh, nothing. Call it a hunch." Finch shook his head and turned to the swaying caretaker. "Show me the... *other* thing, Jim"

"Aye," Jim pointed towards the front doors. "Over here."

Finch squatted down next to the drain and poked the shoe fragment with the tip of the ball-point pen that he had taken from the breast pocket of his ill-fitting black suit.

"Sorry about the puke." Jim slurred. "I'd 'ave done it elsewhere if I'd known the grid was evidence."

Finch grunted distractedly. His attention was fully focused on the corrosive effect the goop was having on the plastic writing implement. He was so engrossed that the sudden yelp from the letterbox nearly gave him a coronary.

"Billy."

Finch looked around. Standing at the window looking absolutely petrified were the pale figures of Fisher, Granger and Paul the plumber.

"There is a bloody shoggoth loose in the building," Fisher bellowed through the metal flap.

"A what?" Jim spluttered.

Finch didn't need to ask. He knew only too well what Fisher meant. "Damn. Where is it now?"

"Second floor, I think. But it's coming for us. We need to get it down in the tunnels and seal it up."

“How?” Finch asked. Panic building up inside his normally unflappable psyche.

“We don't have time for twenty questions, Bill. We need the maintenance key.” Fisher pointed at Jim through the window. “Where is it?”

Jim stuttered. “It's on my kitchen table with the spare flat keys.”

“Gimmie your front-door key... Now.”

Jim did as he was told and posted his keys through the letterbox.

Fisher scooped them up and the three of them raced off in the direction of his humble abode.

“We've got to help them.” Finch shouted. “Let us in.”

Jim looked at him with a pained expression. “I can't.”

“Why the hell not?” Finch was turning red with frustration.

“Because I just gave them the key... It was on the same ring as my flat key.”

“Bollocks,” Finch exploded, then took a couple of deep breaths. “Fielding,” he shouted across the lawn.

Fielding nodded.

“Get the big red key out of the car.”

Again, Fielding nodded and turned in the car's direction.

Jim shrugged. “Big red key?”

Finch smiled. “The battering ram... We'll have to go old-school.”

XII

Jim's flat smelt like a brewery. The ripe fruity aroma of empty beer-cans and half-empty cider bottles hung heavy in the air. It was obvious from just one glance that the caretaker took little care for his own dwelling. It looked like a bomb had hit it. As Fisher charged into the kitchen, he honestly couldn't tell whether the shoggoth had been in there or not, such was the state of disrepair. The keys were where Jim had said. Due to the general state of disorder, Fisher chalked that up as a minor miracle.

"Quick," Paul yelled from the door. "I can hear it on the stairs."

Fisher stopped to grab a bottle of water

from off the side then ran back out into the corridor. “Here.” He passed Granger the water. “Rinse your eyes out.”

She undid the cap and poured the spring water into her eyes. She groaned in relief. “Thanks Sarge.”

Fisher smiled. “Sorry about getting the salt in them in the first place.”

“Hey,” Granger smiled in response. “It was either that or a tentacle in the face. I know which I'd prefer.”

Fisher tossed Paul the keys as he helped Granger clean her eyes. “Get the maintenance door open. I don't know what key it is. You will have to try 'em all.”

Paul took the keys and ran to the far end of the corridor. There were several keys of the right type on the ring. The first three he tried didn't fit but the fourth opened the door. Fisher and Granger caught up with him as the door swung open, revealing a set of concrete steps down into a dark tunnel.

“Good work, Paul.” Fisher slapped him on the back. “I'll go first, pass me your torch.”

Paul took the torch from his tool belt and handed it over.

Crash

"Tekeli-li."

The shoggoth smashed through the staircase door and slammed into the wall opposite. The creature had grown to an enormous size due to all the meals he had eaten that day. The whole building shook from the force of the impact. One of the strip-lights fell from the ceiling and shattered on the floor.

"Run," Granger screamed and pushed Paul through the door. Slamming the door behind her, she leapt down the small flight and collided with Paul.

The shoggoth screeched and slammed into the door, smashing it off its hinges and sending it flying down the steps. It clipped the bottom step and pivoted on one end. Granger cried out "Move," and shoved Paul out of harm's way. Unfortunately, it caught her a glancing blow on the shoulder and sent her sprawling onto the floor.

"Granger," Fisher cried and hauled her upright by the armpits.

The shoggoth spilled down the steps like a river and coalesced at the bottom.

The emergency lighting cast the corridor

in a sickly green glow. The access point to the tunnel was down the far end. Fisher pushed Paul and Granger in front of himself and grabbed a fire extinguisher off the wall. "Go," he commanded. "Find the tunnel." He pulled the pin and gave the incoming creature a sharp blast of freezing cold CO2. It let out a piercing cry and slammed into the ceiling as it tried to get out of the line of fire.

Fisher used this opportunity to back down the corridor and take aim. "Get a sodding move on," he yelled.

Granger had located the hatch in the floor that Sarah had marked on the plans, but the damn thing was stuck. "I'm trying," she yelled in frustration.

The corridor was littered with tools and empty bottles. It was Jim's domain, after all. Looking quickly around, he spotted a crowbar. He grabbed the implement and jammed it in the gap around the hatch. "Kick it," he told Granger. "Do some of your ninja stuff on it."

She stood upright and delivered a stiff stomp to the pivoted crowbar. The hatch flipped open and slammed into the wall. Foul air billowed from the newly opened passage.

"Get in," she told Paul. He lowered himself down and switched on his torch.

The shoggoth soon recovered and sent two thick tentacles out in Fisher's direction. He blasted one with the extinguisher and then the other. They slammed into the walls of the tunnel bringing a hail of rubble down on its back. Fisher gave it the rest of the canister then dropped it and ran.

"That won't hold it for long," Fisher said as he climbed down after Paul and Granger. "We need to find that door."

The ground shook and rumbled as the building started to collapse above them. The shoggoth roared and oozed out from under the debris. It slid along the tunnel and sloshed down the hatch after them.

There was only one choice of direction in the ancient tunnel. One way had been bricked up. Presumably where the original wall had been before Winkleman smashed it down. The other was was a short stretch of tunnel that soon opened out into the vaulted cellar of Edwards Manor.

"There's the door," Granger shouted as she slid into the room. The army had emptied it completely and it was nothing more than a stone box with a door in one wall. The door was only slightly ajar and the seal had fallen to the floor and smashed. Probably due to the vibrations during construction of Burridge Court.

Paul charged across the room and wrenched the door open. Granger and Fisher were about to join him when the shoggoth burst into the room separating them.

Taking the scrimshaw out of his belt, Paul waved it in the air. “Oi, Shoggie,” he yelled. “Is this what you want?”

The building shook again, and a section of ceiling crashed to the floor in the centre of the room, blocking Paul's escape.

Tekeli-li'

A huge orange eye opened in the centre of the shoggoth's body. It glared at Paul then sent a questing tentacle in his direction.

“Paul,” Granger yelled. “Get the hell out of there,”

“No time,” he replied, still waving the scrimshaw. “Seal the damn thing up.” With those final words, he jumped through the open door.

"Paul."

The shoggoth flowed after him, through the doorway and into the tunnel.

"Quick. Seal the fucking door," Fisher bellowed.

"What about Paul?" Granger pleaded. "We can't just leave him."

"He's probably dead already. The whole town will soon be dead if that thing gets loose. So, seal the fucking door.

Granger swallowed her arguments and nodded. She knew that Fisher was right. There was nothing that they could do for Paul now. Nimbly, she climbed over the rubble and took the star-shaped talisman out of her pocket.

With both hands, she slammed the door and shot the bolts. Wedging the talisman in the keyhole, she said a prayer and hoped that it would work.

She quickly re-joined Fisher and they ran back down the tunnel.

"Shit," Fisher said as he noticed that the hatch had dropped. He ran up to it and strained against it... It was no good. Rubble from the collapsing building must have fallen on it, trapping them utterly. "Well," he shrugged.

“Looks like that's it.”

“Yeah,” Granger laughed ironically. “It certainly looks that way... What we need is a miracle...”

Crash

As if on cue, the bricked off tunnel exploded in a shower of dust and rubble as DS Finch smashed it open with one mighty slam of the battering ram.

“Out,” Finch ordered. Fisher and Granger looked at each other in shock then did what they were told.

They followed Finch down the tunnel. Soon, they reached another hatch. Climbing out, they realised that they were in the other block of flats just down the road.

As he stepped out into the rain, Fisher had never been so happy to be outside in his life.

XIII

Fisher and Granger sat on the bonnet of Paul's van watching the fires rage in the pile of wreckage that had been Burridge Court. If DS Finch hadn't remembered about the tunnel, they would have been buried underneath it.

Finch had watched in horror as the glistening mass of the shoggoth flowed from the staircase and chased them down the corridor. He remembered vividly the tunnel uncovered by the builders and also that it ran directly under both blocks of flats. It took only a small leap of faith to convince himself that he could help them by going down from the other block... It was a gamble that had paid off.

Whilst they had been making good their escape, the whole building had come crashing down. Fires broke out and fire-engines were soon on the scene. Fisher had told him that Paul had sacrificed himself to trap the shoggoth. Finch would see to it personally that he got a hero's send off. Fisher was an old pal of the hulking detective and anyone who saved a friend of Finch's was a hero in his book.

As he lit a cigarette, Finch spotted a black car with blacked-out windows pull into the car park. "Here we go..."

“Eh?” Granger asked.

Finch pointed at the car. “I take it that you've never signed the official secrets act before?”

“Nope.” Granger shook her head.

“How about you, Fisher?”

“Nah... You?

Finch sighed. “Many times, I'm afraid.” He looked at the smouldering wreckage thoughtfully. “This damn town...”

“What about the tunnels?” Fisher asked.

Finch cracked his knuckles. "Trust me... I'm going to make damn sure that they are flooded with concrete this time... You can count on it." He set his jaw in a firm line and started to stride across the car park with a purpose.

“I wouldn't want to be whoever's in that car.” Fisher sniggered. “Billy has one hell of a temper on him at times.”

Granger looked up at the column of smoke that spiralled into the night sky. Cinders danced as the fire hoses fought to keep the inferno contained. She was lucky to have survived. So many didn't. She figured that the official like would be some kind of disaster. A gas leak maybe. Soon her lips would be sealed by a government act and she would never be allowed to speak about the events of that horrible day... Not that she would ever want to.

As she counted her blessings, her mind drifted back to poor Paul. She could only hope that his end had been quick...

***

Paul heard the door slam above him. It echoed down the narrow passage as he ran for his life. The gradient was steep, and the centuries of slime made it incredibly slippery. He held out both arms and used the walls to keep upright. He had jammed the scrimshaw into his belt and held the torch in his teeth.

The tunnel was exactly as Crabtree had described. It stunk worse than any drain he had ever encountered. Reaching the bottom of the slope, he heard a noise that chilled his soul...

"Tekeli-li."

It was followed by a ghastly slurping, rushing noise and he knew that the shoggoth was coming for him.

Paul began to sprint for his life. The beam of his flashlight bounced as he raced forwards.

"Tekeli-li."

The shoggoth was mere metres behind him. He could hear the ripples of its monstrous form. Hear the thrashing of its tentacles and the snapping of its maw.

His lungs burned and his eyes streamed as he tried to keep going. He couldn't keep going for much longer.

Suddenly, the tunnel opened out into a colossal underground cavern. It was so vast that his torchlight couldn't reach the roof or outer walls. Paul dived behind a pile of rocks and tried to keep silent.

The shoggoth surged into the cavern and stopped a few feet from Paul's position.

"Tekeli-li," the creature piped.

What Paul heard next shattered what remained of his sanity. "Tekeli-li." "Tekeli-li." "Tekeli-li," hundreds of shoggoth voices piped in reply.

Paul peered around the rocks and shone the light into the gloom as a gelatinous horde came into view.

Paul gibbered and laughed hysterically as they closed in around him. His last thought was a prayer. He prayed that the shoggoths would never get out of their prison. If they did, the world was doomed.

He closed his eyes and switched off the torch as a tentacle reached out for his head...

"Tekeli-li."

ABOUT THE AUTHOR

Tim Mendees is a rather odd chap. He's a horror writer from Macclesfield in the North-West of England that specialises in cosmic horror and weird fiction. A lifelong fan of classic weird tales, Tim set out to bring the pulp horror of yesteryear into the 21st Century and give it a distinctly British flavour. His work has been described as the lovechild of H.P. Lovecraft and P.G. Wodehouse and is often peppered with a wry sense of humour that acts as a counterpoint to the unnerving, and often disturbing, narratives.

Tim has had over eighty published short stories and novelettes along with six stand-alone novellas and a short story collection.

When he is not arguing with the spellchecker, Tim is a goth DJ and a co-host of the Innsmouth Book Club podcast. He currently lives in Brighton & Hove with his pet crab, Gerald, and an army of stuffed octopods.

https://timmendeeswriter.wordpress.com/

https://tinyurl.com/timmendeesyoutube

MORE FROM NORDIC PRESS

NOVELS/NOVELLAS

Face of Fear by C. Marry Hultman
9789198671001

Dawson Junior G3 by Brian Wagstaff
9789198671049

Boy in the Wardrobe by Esther Jacoby
9789198684018

New Life Cottage by Esther Jacoby
9789198671056

The Wait by Esther Jacoby
e-book:https://books2read.com/u/4Dgz8Q

Liebe ist Warten by Esther Jacoby
9789198671070

Das Cottage by Ester Jacoby
9789198684070

Musing on Death & Dying by Esther Jacoby
9789198671063

Earth Door by Cye Thomas
9789198671025

An Odd Collection of Tales By Cye Thomes
9789198684124

Graffiti Stories by Nick Gerrard
9789198671018

Punk Novelette by Nick Gerrard
9789198671087

Struggle and Strife by Nick Gerrard
9789198684049

Fake Escape by Natalie Hughes
e-book:https://books2read.com/u/bMXL5X

Cold as Hell by Neen Cohen
9789198684094

Hell Hath No Fury by Chisto Healy
9789198750706

True Mates by E.F. Vogel
9789198750713

CHRONICLES

Six Days to Hell by E.L. Giles
9789198684087

Murder Planet by Adam Carpenter
9789198671032

Generation Ship by Adam Carpenter
9789198684063

Sunshine by L.T. Emery

Anthologies

Just 13
9789198684025

Lost Lore & Legends
9789198671094

Rise and Fall
9789198750911

www.ingramcontent.com/pod-product-compliance
Ingram Content Group UK Ltd.
Pitfield, Milton Keynes, MK11 3LW, UK
UKHW012250290726
14090UKWH00016B/560

9 789198 750959